PLAYING

POSSUM

by Stephanie Rabig

DEDICATION

I'd like to thank Kealan Patrick Burke for his series of amazing killer-animal covers (including this one); Alan Baxter for writing The Roo and getting this whole ball rolling; and the World Wildlife Fund, my daughter's favorite charity-- all proceeds from this book will be going there.

CHAPTER ONE

Sam wasn't sure it was possible to get drunk enough to deal with this.

Trevor had been saying for a couple of weeks now—roughly half the time they'd been dating—that she just *had* to meet his friends.

Problem was, she'd met a couple of them when they'd come into the Sunny Side Up Diner. They were loud, obnoxious, and shit at tipping.

How had quiet, studious Trevor fallen in with that crowd?

But she couldn't exactly tell him that she'd seen his friends at her coworker Vanessa's table for about twenty minutes total and had already written them off. She knew the golden rule of retail—someone who's rude to the waitstaff isn't even worth a wad of used gum—but they had done what she'd wanted for the past three or four dates. She could suffer through a night out with "bro!" being the most-said word.

Currently, she was nursing a beer while she and Trevor talked to an old school friend of his, Caleb. The four other friends, Huey, Duey, Louey, and—

Be nice, she chided herself.

Michael, Andy, Dylan, and Tanner were playing a game of poker. They of course had made the requisite strip poker jokes, and she and Caleb's girlfriend Alexis—who was currently in the bathroom—had rolled their eyes in unison. The game had gotten sidetracked by Tanner insisting he could do magic tricks, and subsequently dropping half the pack on the floor.

"Dammit," he muttered, somehow managing to slur a word that didn't have any 's's. "Help me pick these up."

Sam started to say something else to Trevor and then froze as she heard a word from the table that did not belong anywhere near a white person's mouth. Beside her, Trevor bit his lip and Caleb sighed loudly. Whether at the word or her clearly poor reaction to it, she didn't know. Wasn't going to take the time to ask, either.

"What was that?" she asked, glaring around at the four of them. Michael looked away, Tanner didn't seem to have realized she'd spoken, and Andy was trying to open another beer. Dylan's smile, however, turned into something defensive and mean.

"You heard me," he said, holding up one of the aces. "It's a spade, see? That means it's a—"

"Do *not* say it again," she said, looking to Trevor for backup.

He didn't provide any. Caleb just sighed again and said, "It's just how they talk when they're drunk. Ignore it, they're dumbasses."

"You're the dumbass!" Dylan shot back, and apparently this was considered the height of humor because they all cackled like hyenas and then started throwing insults back and forth.

"Right," Sam said. "I'm gonna go get some air."

She set down her half-full beer and walked out of the trailer, moving off the porch to stand out on the lawn. A moment later, Trevor came out to join her.

"I'm sorry," he said, wrapping his arms around her. "They get that way sometimes. They don't mean anything by it, Sam. It's just how they were raised. I mean, you should hear their parents."

"I don't really want to."

"C'mon," he said, in that cajoling tone that she normally found cute. "Let's go back inside."

Right, she thought. So she could keep drinking and wishing that they'd just gone to dinner instead, and Dylan could find ways to needle his friend's new stick-in-the-mud girlfriend?
"I think I just want to go home."

"Sam, no. Don't be like that. I've really been looking forward to you meeting the guys. Let's not ruin it, huh?"

"Who exactly is ruining anything?" she asked, taking a step back and crossing her arms. "Because it's not me."

"I told you, they didn't mean anything by it. It was just a stupid joke. They're good guys; they're not racist. In fact, in high school, Tanner's best friend was—"

"Please. I am literally begging you not to finish that sentence," she groaned. "Just go on back in, okay? I'll talk to you tomorrow.''

Maybe, she thought, digging her keys out of her jeans pocket and stalking over to her car.

"Sam!" he exclaimed. "Hey, come on!"

"Ohhhh!" Dylan yelled from out the window. She wondered how long he'd been listening. "Someone's not getting any tonight!"

"Shut up, Dylan!" Trevor yelled back.

So *that* gets a response, Sam thought. She turned on the engine and started to back out of the driveway, checking the rearview and then returning her focus to Trevor, hoping he would react, would tell Dylan off and ask her to wait.

Instead, he stared after her, glancing back at the porch when Caleb opened the door for him. Then he turned and went back inside. She fancied she could hear him joining in with the others' laughter as she pulled out into the street.

Asshole. No wonder Alexis had retreated to the bathroom so fast.

She was four blocks away when the insecurity hit.

Maybe she'd overreacted. What had she expected him to do, throw a punch at someone he'd been friends with since third grade? She'd seen them at the diner and seen them drunk; Trevor had known them for over a decade. He knew them in a way she didn't. And here she'd been dating him for a month and thought she could dictate who he hung out with?

"No," she said, her voice loud in the car. "No, that is bullshit."

She hadn't expected him to punch Dylan. But a simple "not cool" wouldn't have been difficult.

Her phone rang, making her flinch. Trevor's ringtone.

She sighed and disconnected it from the charger. "What?"

"Where are you?"

"A couple of minutes from home."

"Shit," he said. "I thought maybe you were just circling the block."

"No."

"Sure you don't want to come back?"

"Did you say anything to Dylan?"

He hesitated a little too long, and she could picture him on the other end of the phone, rubbing at the back of his neck the way he did when he was nervous.

"Bye, Trevor."

She ended the call and dropped the phone into the passenger seat.

A few seconds later it rang again, and she swore, casting it a quick glare. Should've put the damn thing on silent while—

Something bumped under her front left tire.

Cursing again, she pulled off the road. She knew better; she knew better than to take her eyes off this stretch of road for even a second. There were trees on either side in the run up to her house, and she'd seen deer bounding across here countless times. She was just lucky she hadn't hit one of them.

Getting out of the car, she looked back, using her cell phone flashlight to illuminate the road.

It was a possum. She'd slowed down to talk to Trevor, and so the poor thing wasn't dead like it might've been had she been going the speed limit.

"Shit," she whispered. It was trying to drag itself back into the trees. Its back two legs were shattered at the very least; it would die without help.

Her father had grown up in an even smaller town than this, just in Oklahoma. She remembered how he'd carried a pistol in his truck in case of wild hogs, and how he'd talked about mercy killing a deer once that hadn't died on impact with his vehicle.

She didn't think she had that in her.

"Okay, just—just hang on a minute," she said, feeling ridiculous because of course the little animal couldn't understand her. She got back into her car and drove the last half-block to her house, hurrying inside and grabbing a thick towel. She would wrap it up in that, because no way was she actually going to touch it. Did these things carry rabies? She couldn't remember.

Didn't matter, she thought. You hit it, so you take care of it. You can call the vet in the morning and see what they might be able to do.

She tried to jam her cell phone into her pants

pocket, but it stuck halfway out and she left it on the table near the front door instead and grabbed a small flashlight. That, at least, she could hold in her teeth instead of using her hands.

As she opened the front door, Trevor's ringtone sounded again and she closed the door behind her firmly. Whatever excuses he had now could just wait.

She hurried down the tree-lined road, pressing the button on the bottom of the flashlight and holding it in her mouth. She caught up with the possum just as it reached the edge of the pavement.

"Oh no you don't," she mumbled, but though she told herself to just reach out and wrap it in the towel, now that she was close enough to really see it, to smell the stink of it and see the shine of the blood trail, suddenly she wasn't sure if this was a good idea.

But what else was she going to do? Kill it? Walk away and leave it to die a slow death?

She could almost hear her mother's voice— "Might not be the nicest thing to do, but it's the wisest."

Well, her mom had always been a lot more pragmatic. Taking a deep breath—and immediately regretting it because really, that *smell*—she ducked down and draped the towel over the possum, gingerly pushing it onto its side and trying to wrap it up like a burrito.

To say this displeased the possum would be to say football fans get a little energetic during the Super Bowl.

It hissed and squirmed, its dry, snakelike tail lashing

around like a whip.

"Settle down!" Sam said, trying to keep her voice calm as she spoke around the flashlight. "I'm trying to help you."

It nosed out of the front part of the towel and hissed again, going for her hand as she tried to regain her grip on it.

She realized what it was doing, but not in time, and its teeth sank into her index finger.

"Ow!" she yelped, the flashlight falling from her mouth. It rolled on the pavement, illuminating a bloody towel and glistening sharp teeth. "You little asshole!"

Rabies, she thought. Tetanus, lockjaw, AIDS—

No, not AIDS, you dumbass.

She laughed at herself, short and a little hysterical. Whatever the diseases might be, she needed to disinfect this *now*.

"Fine!" she said, as the possum lay at the edge of the ditch, its dirty white fur bristling as it growled at her. It would've looked pretty damn intimidating if it wasn't for the broken back legs. "Go off and die of thirst or something!"

It growled again. She started to reach down and grab the flashlight and the towel, but then she decided she'd risked enough digits for one evening and just turned to go back to her house.

Over a dozen possums were standing in the road.

"What the hell…" she whispered, the words barely

audible from her suddenly-dry mouth. She took a step back and the wounded possum scrambled forward, pulling itself close enough on its front legs to bite her ankle. Sam shrieked, kicking her foot out and sending the animal flying. She leaned over to check the damage to her leg and heard the dry shuffling of a multitude of animals moving closer.

She raised her head, and they stopped.

"Nope," she murmured, feeling more of the hysterical laughter bubbling up. "No, no no. Screw this."

Her car was back at the house. Phone was there, too.

So don't go for your house, she thought. Head back to Caleb's. Trevor can take you to the hospital.

She turned, and though she didn't see any possums in the road, she saw eyes shining at her from off in the trees. A lot of them.

Leaning down slowly, she grabbed the flashlight and waved it around, searching the ditch. She saw three possums right away, their fat little bodies pressed tight to the ground, mouths open in horrifying Vs to show their teeth.

She grabbed for a tree branch at the side of the road and the possums in the ditch immediately went for her, and this wasn't *right*; possums were supposed to play dead or something, not attack, and they sure as hell didn't hunt in packs!

You go right ahead, then, and tell them that this

isn't logical, she thought wildly, swinging the branch. It connected with two of the animals, but the third got in under the swing, biting her leg. She screamed and kicked it away, then slammed the branch into its back, feeling an awful, sharp sense of triumph at the satisfying crunch. She raised the branch again, only for three others to come at her. And then five others. And then eight.

Back in Sam痴 house, the phone began to ring again.

CHAPTER TWO

"Hey, Ness. How was work?"

Vanessa groaned, untying her long hair from the bun she wore it in at the Sunny Side Up Diner. Normally she loved the feeling of letting her hair down, but today she'd been dashing all over the place, sweating, and working over the fryer. It felt like her hair was one greasy black lump. "Awful. I had to wait double the tables because Sam didn't show up."

John frowned. "That doesn't sound like her. Isn't Carlie the one who skips all the time?"

"Yeah, but she got fired for that a couple of weeks ago. Sam doesn't usually pull that sh—" Her uncle cast a pointed look at Sophia, who was sitting at her laptop and typing frantically, and Vanessa cleared her throat. "Stuff. Either of you need in the bathroom? I'm gonna take a shower."

"I'm good."

"Sophia?" She grinned and moved closer to her cousin. "Hey, Soph. Earth calling."

"Huh?"

"You need to get in the bathroom before I shower?"

"No, no, go ahead."

"What's got you all riled up? Arguing on Facebook again?"

"Sophia," John groaned. "Your mother has to work

with these people."

"Well that doesn't mean they can just sit around being stupid!" Sophia protested. "Look at this!" She scooted back and pointed indignantly at the screen, where someone had posted a picture of a possum to the town's page. "Mrs. Thompson took this—she said it would've bitten her ankle if she hadn't made it to her car, and that she bets it was rabid! Do you know how rare it is for possums to get rabies? Their body temperature is all wrong! Besides, they eat ticks, which *are* an actual problem! She probably just startled the poor thing."

"Did you tell her that?" Vanessa said, smiling as she saw that one of the comments was a wall of text from Sophia. "That and more, looks like. What's the video you sent?"

"There's trappers on YouTube, who get animals out of people's attics and stuff? This guy shows how it's near impossible to provoke a possum into biting you. They're sweethearts. You know, if one gets hit, you actually really should check the body around this time of year to make sure there aren't babies."

"You didn't tell her *that*, did you?"

"Yeah, why?"

Vanessa nodded to the screen, where Mrs. Thompson's reply had come up.

"Like hell am I going near roadkill!"

Sophia let out a frustrated groan. "I give her all that information and she doesn't even say anything about it?

Just gets grossed out over one thing? The babies wouldn't even be roadkill; they would need help!"

She started to type a response, and John took her hands. "That's enough. Even if you didn't get her to listen, other people'll read that and learn something. Okay? No point arguing with her."

"But she's such a dumbass!"

"Sophia."

"Sorry, dad. But—"

He gave her his patented Look Of Parental Disappointment, and Vanessa winced in sympathy. She'd been on the receiving end of those a time or three since he and Aunt Becca had taken her in seven years ago.

"Okay, okay," Sophia said, turning off her laptop.

"Isn't it about time for your shift, anyway?" Vanessa asked.

Sophia frowned, then looked at her cell phone, grimacing when she saw the time. Every weekday, she volunteered at the animal shelter from 4:30 to 5:30. It was 4:26. "Gotta go!"

"Get a protein bar!" John admonished, and Sophia ran to the cupboard, grabbing a bar and sticking it in her mouth, wrapper and all, as she tugged on her shoes. Then she pulled off the wrapper, tossing it in the trash on her way out the door.

"I never should've told her she could get a Facebook account," John sighed. "At least on Instagram she just follows puppy and kitten accounts. And National

Geographic. That's fine. But…"

"Hey, the sooner she learns how to handle idiots online, the sooner she'll be ready for the wonderful world of retail."

He winced at that, and she gave him a commiserating pat on the shoulder. "I know. I don't want to think about her working Black Friday someday either. Rite of passage nowadays, I guess."

"I guess. At least things don't get as crazy here as they do in the cities."

"True. Though there was that time Tiffany had to call security on one of the Stewart kids for climbing a display to get the last TV."

"Didn't he break his arm doing that?"

"No, Jake lost a tooth when he fell. The broken arm was Tim, jumping off that boxcar in the park."

"Oh yeah."

"Anyway, I'm gonna shower before Aunt Becca gets home." She'd had to work overtime—a not-uncommon occurrence for the chief of police, even in a town this small—and her preferred routine afterwards was a long soak in the tub.

"Don't fall down the drain," John said absently, and Vanessa groaned as she went to get a change of clothes. She would've thought the Dad Jokes would stop once Sophia reached her teen years, but no. Apparently they were eternal.

Just when she was about to step into the shower, her

phone chirped.

Tiffany, she thought, smiling as she opened the text.

"Hey. Rain check on dinner; working til 11 tnght."

Damn, Vanessa thought. She typed back, "Tomorrow?"

"Should work! Sry."

"Here I was showering for you and everything."

"Lucky me. I know how rare that is."

Vanessa laughed. "Brat."

"And you looooove meeee."

"I do. See you tomorrow!"

She set an alarm for 10:58—she knew it was paranoid of her, but whenever Tiffany got off work after dark she liked to talk to her on the way to her car—and then got into the shower.

~~*

Tiffany groaned as she walked out of Walmart, trying to pretend that her 'walk' didn't resemble 'staggering like a zombie'. She wanted to sag in relief after that long day but knew her back would definitely not allow it.

She prided herself on her strength, but hauling boxes around in the stockroom would take it out of anyone after a while. It was definitely going to be a heating-pad-and-aspirin night.

Hopefully she'd feel better tomorrow. If Vanessa caught her grimacing at dinner, she'd insist on making another chiropractor appointment for her. It helped, yeah, but since she was part-time she didn't get health insurance and it was $75 a visit.

Vanessa insisted it was no problem, that she knew Tiffany would do the same for her, but it still made her feel guilty to see Ness spend part of her paycheck like that.

Her phone rang then, and Tiffany pulled it out of her pocket, smiling as she answered. "Hello, Miss Panicky."

"Shush," Vanessa laughed. "You know the one time I don't call, something'll happen."

"No, I don't know that. *You* know that. This is what happens when you watch too much Unsolved Mysteries as a kid."

"Hey, I don't have to watch Unsolved Mysteries to know that dark parking lots are creepy."

"I think they're nice," Tiffany said, looking up. She wanted to see the stars, but the tall lamps in the parking lot were blocking them out, and all she could see was the glow of halogen lights and the swarm of bugs around each one. "Actually, it'd be nicer if they *were* actually dark." She drew closer to her car, then paused. "Huh. That's weird."

"What?"

"I think there's an animal under my car. No, wait…there's two or three."

"Probably some stray cats."

"Or the raccoons have finally organized."

Vanessa laughed. "I still don't know what you have

against poor raccoons. They're cute."

"They have creepy little hands!" Pressing the phone to her ear with her shoulder, Tiffany clapped. "Shoo! Go on!"

"Did they leave?"

"No, hang on. I'm gonna use the phone light; that'll scare them off." She shone the flashlight under the car from several feet away, and then held it up to her ear again. "It's possums."

"Really? Well, at least it's not skunks."

"Or raccoons."

"Or raccoons," Vanessa echoed, and she could easily picture the smile on her face.

"They're close to the driver's side door; I'm just gonna climb in on the passenger side. Don't want them to think my toes are mice or something. What do possums eat, anyway?"

"Not sure."

"Doesn't matter. They'll run as soon as I start the engine."

Tiffany walked around to the other side of the car and shrieked, her phone and car keys falling from her hand. Crouched on the other side of the car were at least a dozen more possums.

She could vaguely hear Vanessa's voice, calling her name, demanding to know what was wrong. She tried to speak; tried to explain; couldn't get enough air for any words. She just turned and ran.

She only made it about a dozen feet before the first set of teeth pierced her ankle.

~~*

"Aunt Becca!" Vanessa cried, throwing open the door to her aunt and uncle's room. "Get everybody to the Walmart parking lot; Tiffany's in trouble."

She didn't wait for a reply before she was running, clambering into her car and backing out of the driveway, still in her nightgown and bare feet.

It was 25 mph in town and she was going double that by the time she reached Walmart. Her aunt must have sent out the call before she was even out the door, because there was already a cop car there, the lights flashing, and she could hear the wail of an ambulance siren in the distance.

Then a loud bang made her flinch. Had that been a gunshot?

Another followed, then two more, and she ran toward the police car, mindless of the little bits of gravel digging into her bare feet, waving her arms and yelling so as not to accidentally look like a target.

The officer, Jason Murphy, swung his gun toward her for one heart-stopping instant and then lowered it.

She barely even noticed. Tiffany was lying behind him, bleeding.

"Tiffany!" She dropped to her side, gingerly

touching her face. Tiffany didn't move. "What happened? Who did this? Who were you shooting at?"

"Not who, what," Officer Murphy said. "Those things. I think they went rabid or something."

He pointed at the ground, where two possums lay dead. She heard some faint hissing from off in the grass, and thought she saw another animal or two waddling away, but then they were gone, disappearing as the ambulance pulled into the parking lot.

"Tiffany. Hey. Wake up!" None of the wounds looked very deep—from the look of her hands, they'd gotten the worst of it. She'd been able to defend herself that much, anyway, and had kept them largely away from her throat.

She wasn't going to bleed out. The clinic was less than ten minutes away; she'd be fine.

And it'd be a lot easier to tell herself all this if Tiffany would just open her eyes.

But she didn't, even as she was loaded onto the ambulance. Her blood shone dark on the asphalt where she'd been lying, and Vanessa looked away, feeling worse than helpless.

Then she caught sight of something gleaming on the ground. Tiffany's keys. And her cell phone, the screen shattered.

God, she was gonna be pissed. She hated spending money.

Vanessa didn't even realize she was crying until her

aunt came up beside her, wiping at her tears and then pulling her into a hug.

"Come on. I'll take you home; we'll get your car in the morning. Right now you come back and get dressed, and then I'll run you out to the clinic."

Vanessa sniffled and nodded, feeling for all the world like she was fifteen again, startled by a tight hug from a woman who until that point had just been someone she'd seen in Christmas cards and an occasional Facebook video.

Her aunt kissed the top of her head—though now she had to stand a little on tiptoe to do it instead of lean down—and led her to the car.

CHAPTER THREE

"Hey," Vanessa said, feeling most of the tension finally drain from her shoulders when Tiffany opened her eyes. "How're you feeling?"

"Like shit," Tiffany groaned. She tried to stretch, which didn't work so well on account of the IV, and then her eyes widened. "Goddammit. Come on," she said, raising her voice. "Hey! Unhook this stupid thing! I can't be in here," she muttered. "Fucking hospitals. There's no way I can afford all this. How long have I been—"

"Overnight," Vanessa said, standing up and resting a hand on her shoulder in lieu of taking her bandaged hand. "It's okay. We'll—"

"It is not okay! What the hell happened? Did you drive me? Please say yes, say I'm not on the hook for an ambulance ride."

"I didn't know what was happening; I just heard you scream. I'm sorry."

Tiffany waved as best she could with her free hand. "No, no. Not your fault. Hell, I hate to think what kind of shape I'd be in if you hadn't called. Last thing I remember I got…I got bitten," she said, inspecting the bandages up and down her arms. The off-white color of the bandages, along with the pale yellow of the hospital gown, seemed to transfer a sallowness to her black skin. The hollows under her eyes didn't help matters; it seemed like she'd lost ten pounds and most of her energy overnight.

"A lot," Vanessa said. "They think you surprised a mom with her babies or something. Jason shot a couple of them; they're going to send the bodies in for testing to make sure they don't have anything bad. Even if they do, though, I think you're more antibiotic than blood by now."

"Great," Tiffany said, her head flopping back onto the pillow as the nurse, Joyce, came in.

"When can I go home?" Tiffany asked by way of greeting.

"Ideally, we'd like to keep you one more night, just to—"

"No."

"Tiffany," Vanessa pleaded. "What if something goes wrong?"

"Then my house is six blocks that way," Tiffany said. When Vanessa didn't respond, she sighed. "I'll stay until dinner, okay? Not through dinner, I'll pick up something on the way home, but just until."

"As your highness demands," Joyce said, giving her a wink. In response, Tiffany stuck her tongue out at her.

Vanessa smiled. "I take it you two know each other?"

"Back when I worked as a night cashier, Joyce'd always come in after her shift," Tiffany said. "I was constantly surprised by how much alcohol this one woman could put away…"

"Hush," Joyce said, laughing as she looked over her

vitals. "I bought no such thing."

"Okay, okay. It might have been a nightly Snickers."

"That's more like it. Everything checks out so far," she said, stepping back and checking the level in the IV drip bag. "How're you feeling? Any dizziness, nausea?"

"No."

"Good. Now I'll make a note on your chart—no dinner, you want to be gone before then." She lowered her voice. "If you're worried about the cost, I'll get together some financial aid forms for you to take home."

"Thanks so much, Joyce."

"Anytime, sweetie. Now you get some rest. Vanessa? Your uncle's here."

"I'll be right back," Vanessa said, heading out of Tiffany's small room and into the main waiting area. "Hey, Uncle John."

"How's she doing?"

"Okay. They're supposed to let her out tonight before dinner."

"That soon?"

"Yeah, well, time is money and all that."

He nodded. "I talked to your boss; she knows you won't be in today. And Aunt Becca talked to the manager out at Walmart."

"Thanks."

"You need anything?"

"Some lunch after while?" she asked, glancing at

the clock. 8:24.

"Will do."

"So what's the paper?"

"Oh, this," he said, smiling sheepishly as he held it out. "Sophia made a get-well card."

Vanessa stared at it, eyebrows raised. The bottom half of the sheet of paper was covered with a printed-out collage of opossums; none with their teeth showing, all looking roly-poly and adorably big-eyed. On the top half, Sophia had drawn a speech balloon with 'We're sorry!' in it.

"It is cute," Vanessa said. "But…"

"Yeah, I don't know how well she'll take to pictures of them right now," John said. "You can give at your own discretion, I guess."

"Tell her thanks."

"Here," John said, digging a ten-dollar bill out of his wallet. "Get the two of you something from the cafeteria to tide you over until lunch."

"Thanks."

"And get some water, too. No—"

"—dehydration on your watch. I know."

"Exactly."

He smiled as he said it, but she remembered the scare he'd gotten the summer after she'd moved down. Aunt Becca had been working the local craft fair, and had gotten busy enough talking to people and keeping on top of various complaints and requests that she'd passed out from heatstroke. Nothing like that had ever happened again, but her uncle had still gotten a little obsessive over having a water bottle handy at all times.

"I'll be back around noon," he said, and she was suddenly overcome with the urge to hug him, and too tired from staying up at Tiffany's bedside to try and argue with herself.

He went still with surprise for a few seconds, and then hugged her back. "It's okay," he said. "She's gonna be fine."

"I know," she said. "Just…thanks."

"Of course," he said, with the quiet puzzlement that was always there whenever she fought through the self-consciousness enough to try to be sincere about everything.

When she was fifteen, her dad had thrown her out after going through her email and finding her messages to a classmate. They hadn't even been that bad—no nudes or anything, just some mild flirting. But they had been sent to another girl, and that had been enough.

Her dad had broken her phone in the ensuing argument, so she'd called Uncle John, her father's brother, from a nearby gas station. And he hadn't asked questions, hadn't tried to talk out whether or not there was somewhere else she could go. He'd just told her to stay put, and then driven the eleven hours to come get her.

(The employee at the 24-hour gas station who'd let her use the phone told his manager what was going on when she'd come on shift, which was how she'd gotten temporarily adopted by said manager and three other employees, one of whom was also a lesbian and had some *very* choice words about her dad.)

Uncle John had pulled into the gas station and looked her over, then asked if she had any of her things. When she'd said no, he'd talked to the manager for a few moments, and then told her he would be right back.

Almost forty minutes later, he'd pulled back in, the trunk and most of the backseat full with her belongings. She'd asked what he'd said to his brother, asked what her dad had said back.

He'd told her not to worry about it. Which was, she'd come to realize, his philosophy when it came to things like this. Yes, he'd had to give up his home office to create a bedroom for her; yes, they'd had to put off a family vacation they'd been planning for the summer because there was another mouth to feed now…but it was the right thing to do so that was all there was to it. Don't worry about it. And don't thank me, Ness, no getting all weepy; I'm your uncle, what was I supposed to do?

"Anyway, I'd better get back in there," Vanessa said, stepping back. "I leave her alone for too long and she'll go into a Food Network spiral. See you in a few hours."

She turned and hurried back to Tiffany's room, wiping her eyes once she was out of his sight.

That was all seven years ago; normally thinking about it didn't hit her so hard.

Well, having your girlfriend survive a wild-animal attack'll kick in the feelings, I guess, she thought. Then she glanced down at the card in her hand. Could possums even really be considered 'wild animals'? The phrase had always conjured bears and deer and such; bigger things than these fluffy white basketballs.

She went into Tiffany's room and smiled as she sat down. "Uncle John gave me some money for the cafeteria; you up for eating yet?"

"Yeah, some fruit or something. Thanks."

"And Sophia made you a get well card," Vanessa said. "Not really sure you want to see it, though. How do you feel about pictures of possums?"

"What?" Tiffany asked, fumblingly taking the paper with her bandaged hand. She blinked at it a few times, and then started laughing. "Oh my god. I can't believe your cousin. Now I'm just picturing those little assholes bringing me flowers and some balloons."

Vanessa grinned at the weird mental image, then got to her feet. "I'll go get some fruit."

"Hang on," Tiffany said. "Did my phone make it?"

"No," Vanessa said. "Sorry."

"Dammit," Tiffany muttered. "Can I borrow yours?"

Vanessa had her phone halfway out of her purse before Tiffany could even ask. "Back in a few."

"Thanks."

Vanessa dawdled in the cafeteria, trying to give

Tiffany plenty of time to talk to whoever it was she was contacting. After they started dating, there'd never been any question as to whose family they'd spend holidays with. Tiffany had never suggested that she bring Vanessa to meet her parents or any other relatives; Vanessa had never even heard her reference any of them. It was as if she'd just floated into town three years ago like Aphrodite on her shell; her entire past dissolving into so much sea foam.

It had piqued Aunt Becca's curiosity something fierce for a while, but there'd never been any of the pointed questions at the dinner table that Vanessa had worried about when she'd first brought her over.

"Maybe she's just a private person," her aunt had said, when she'd thanked her for not interrogating her new girlfriend. "I hope so. But I also know what happened with you."

They'd dropped the subject then (or rather Vanessa had come up with an excuse to head back to her room). Even now, when she thought about her dad for more than a few glancing seconds, her instinct was to retreat.

But maybe that was natural, instead of some kind of flaw to overcome. Maybe the heart wasn't meant to know how to handle loving and hating someone at the same time.

People tended to assume that since her father had thrown her out, everything had been awful up until that point: that he'd been abusive at least verbally if not physically; that they'd never gotten along. But that wasn't the truth of it. She'd loved her father dearly, and he'd loved her. At least she'd thought that he had.

They'd had their arguments, the biggest one until That Night being the one where he'd confronted her about barely showing up for church anymore. In the end, she'd made up exhaustion that wasn't there, exaggerated the difficulty of her classes, all to avoid telling him that the lectures at the conservative-leaning church she'd grown up in were making her more and more uncomfortable.

Hell, if she'd admitted the truth then, maybe she could've gotten thrown out at twelve instead of fifteen.

But she'd made up excuses instead. And he'd sympathized, offered to help her more with her homework, told her that he loved how diligent she was with her chores but that he would gladly do everything around the house himself if it meant she could keep up with both her studies and her faith.

He'd meant it. He'd taken away her chores entirely—no more dishes, laundry, dusting, or cooking two dinners a week—and she'd continued going to church. She had attended services with him on the morning of their big fight.

Ever since she could remember, other kids she'd brought over had talked about how much they loved her dad, how much they wished their own parents were more like him. He'd loved her.

Hadn't he?

And that was what gnawed, at odd moments when she saw a father and daughter walking around the park; at 3 in the morning when sleep proved impossible; on her dad's birthday. Had he simply been pretending the entire time? Or had he honestly loved her, and parental love—the strongest emotion that humans were supposed to feel, the thing that let mothers lift entire cars off of trapped children—was really that conditional?

Either way…

She missed him.

The knowledge infuriated her, shamed her. It was something she could never say to her aunt and uncle, who'd sacrificed so much to take her in. How could she ever admit she was that ungrateful, that she'd stayed up some nights wishing that she'd had a crush on a Louis instead of on Louise, that she could still call him and complain when she'd had a bad day?

That she could call him right now, when a part of her ached to hear his voice, telling her that everything was going to be fine.

It was the tone he'd used when pulling out a bee stinger from her foot; when she'd forgotten her lines in the school play and just stared out into the audience, frozen; when Patricia had loudly told her that she wasn't invited to her birthday party that weekend because 'your lunches smell funny and so do you'. She wanted to hear that tone again, *needed* to, now that she'd seen her girlfriend's blood on the ground.

But her father's number was still in her phone. In the past seven years, he hadn't called her once.

"Miss? You all right?"

She flinched, nearly dropping the food she was carrying. "Huh?"

"You've been staring at that apple for the past five minutes," the cafeteria worker said. "Doing okay?"

"Yeah. Yeah, I'm fine." She brought the apples, bananas, and container of strawberries up to the register, paying for them quickly and then hurrying back to Tiffany's room before her emotions could catch up with her again. Clearly, the last thing she needed right now was to be alone.

"Hey," Tiffany said, not looking up from the phone. "Snack run successful?"

"Yep," Vanessa said, scooting the side tray over and piling the fruits on it. "Get everybody called?"

Tiffany raised an eyebrow. "Not calling anybody. Just trying to find a link I had saved."

"Oh. So what's the link?"

"Just something," Tiffany said, holding the phone too tightly in one bandaged hand before she set it down next to her and picked up an apple. "These are good," she said, after she'd taken a bite, her free hand still resting possessively over the phone. "Sometimes I get those apples that are just a little mushy, and—"

"Tiff. Is something wrong?"

Tiffany sighed and put the apple down, picking up the phone in a more relaxed grip. "No. Nothing's wrong. I'm fine, just...I guess just a little nervous. A lot's happened."

"It has," Vanessa agreed.

"And it got me thinking. I mean, I teased you about being paranoid and all that but I actually really like that you call me whenever I'm on night shift. And if you hadn't, I…hell, the odds of getting attacked by animals have to be really damn low but what if it had been a person or something? Or if it had been a bear instead of possums?"

"I don't think Kansas has bears," Vanessa said, but she scooted closer, her expression understanding.

"The point is, what if I hadn't made it? Or if something happens to me tomorrow, or to you?"

"You can't start thinking like that," Vanessa said. "You'll drive yourself crazy."

"Or maybe I finally drove myself to some common sense," Tiffany said. "I've been saving up. But with medical bills now, I'm not sure when I'll be able to actually buy it. I just know I don't want to keep holding off asking."

She turned the phone around then, and Vanessa saw that the screen was open to an Etsy window. She managed to take in the scrolled designs on the silver base of the engagement ring and the emerald—her birthstone—before her eyes were swimming with tears again.

"They make a bunch of different designs. This one's just my favorite. But if it sells before I can get it, we'll pick one out together. If…if you want to, I mean? Will you marry me?"

Vanessa nodded, throwing her arms around her

(barely remembering to be mindful of the IV). "Yes. Yes, of course, yes."

~~*

"How're you feeling?" Vanessa asked, as the clock crept closer to lunchtime. "I know you want out of here, but if you'd rather stay in and order a pizza tonight or something that's—"

"You want to have an engagement dinner, don't you."

"Maybe?" Vanessa said, grinning. "I just know I am *not* going to be able to keep this secret."

"Really? I mean, I thought it was super subtle the way you shoved the phone in Joyce's face…"

Vanessa laughed. "Seriously, if you want to do it later that's fine. I just think it'd be really nice to tell everybody at once."

"I'm feeling fine," Tiffany said. Even if she hadn't been, there was no way she'd deny Vanessa something as simple as dinner after the fright she'd had. Yeah, she'd been the one those creepy little bastards had bitten, but Ness had been the one holding vigil at her bedside all night. She'd known Vanessa to go into panic spirals over much smaller things than someone she loved ending up hurt.

Besides, Vanessa was more tied to tradition than she wanted to admit. There was a part of her girlfriend—fiancee, she corrected with a little thrill—that wanted the floofy white dress and rehearsal dinner toasts and her dad walking her down the aisle.

She couldn't give her most of that—the white dress would be something from clearance, not the window displays; the rehearsal dinner would probably be at Chili's or something; and Ness's dad…

No, she couldn't give her everything. Couldn't even come close. So whatever did happen to be in her power, the answer would always be yes.

John rapped on the door then, and Tiffany gave him an honest smile. While she was Ness's first serious relationship, she herself had dated before, and had grown used to two main reactions from her girlfriends' families: awkward half-acceptance, or outright hostility.

If she'd ended up loving any of those girls the way that she loved Vanessa, she would've gladly put up with even the hostility. But she was glad that she'd wound up with someone whose family she genuinely liked.

They were *engaged*.

"Lunch," John said, handing them each a brown paper bag. "Nothing fancy, but I did sneak in some Reese's for you."

"Thanks!" Vanessa exclaimed, going past the sandwich and protein bar and heading straight for the chocolate.

Tiffany echoed her thank-you, and then went on. "I'm going over the wall in a few hours," she said with a grin. "And Vanessa suggested we all go out to dinner.

Kindof a 'yay, I'm alive, and don't want to do dishes tonight' celebration?"

"I think we can swing that," John said. "I'll talk to Rebecca. Where are you thinking of going?"

"Mexican," Tiffany said. "I want to stuff my face with enchiladas until they have to roll me out."

Which was, she was surprised to realize, the truth. Normally when she was sick or cooped up for a while, she lost her appetite, but right now she felt ravenous.

She eyed Vanessa's lunch as well, wondering if she intended to eat all of it.

"Los Amigos is closed on Mondays," John said. "Carlota's work for you, or do you want to go out of town?"

"Carlota's is great."

CHAPTER FOUR

"Excuse me? Vanessa, right?"

Vanessa nodded. The young man who'd just come into the diner looked familiar, but she couldn't quite put a name to the face.

Which wasn't that uncommon a thing in a town this size. She was probably just used to seeing him at wherever he worked and was having a problem placing him without a uniform.

"Have you heard anything from Sam?"

That was why he looked familiar. He met Sam at the end of her shift sometimes. Trevor, Sam had said.

"No," she said. "She just stopped coming in."

"We had a fight," Trevor said, looking ashamed. "I called and called, and then I went by her house—her car's there, her phone, her clothes…"

She raised her eyebrows. "I'm assuming she gave you a key?"

"Yeah, yeah, I'm not a creep," he said. "I thought maybe—you know, that she fell getting out of the shower or something. So I went in and looked through the house, but…"

"How long has it been since you heard from her?"

"We fought Friday night."

And she hadn't come in or even called today, Vanessa thought. So she'd been missing for four days.

"What was the fight about?"

"Vanessa!" Mrs. Hernandez called, nodding to a table that had just been seated—two regulars, Jeanne-Marie Broussard and her granddaughter, Henriette.

Se waved to her boss in acknowledgment. Why had she been starting to question him? Her aunt was the cop, not her.

"I haven't seen her," she said, "but you might go to the police and ask to talk to Aunt Becca—talk to the chief," she corrected. "I've mentioned Sam before; she knows she hasn't been to work. She'll help."

"Thanks," Trevor said, though he'd looked a little ill ever since she'd said the word 'police'.

No wonder, she thought as she walked over to the new table and withdrew her notebook from her apron. Right now, Sam was just pissed at him and had done something impulsive, maybe skipped town for a few days with friends. Getting the police involved meant that it could be much more serious than that.

Then Trevor scurried up to her as she was starting to take orders. "Sorry, sorry," he said. "I just realized—I heard about what happened to Tiffany. I'm glad she's okay."

"So am I," Vanessa said.

He gave the table a quick smile of apology and then left, but the subject had already been changed.

"Tiffany?" Jeanne-Marie said, in lieu of answering what dressing she wanted on her salad. "You mean Tiffany

Campbell? She works at Walmart with my great-granddaughter! I heard she got attacked in the parking lot the other night. Poor thing. How do you know her?"

"She's my fiancee," she said, her pride in the words tempered by the worry of how the two women might react. Jeanne-Marie had always seemed like a sweetheart—as opposed to her twin, Baptiste, who had all the waitresses drawing straws to see who had to deal with him—but she'd never brought up a subject like this with her or Henriette.

Blessedly, Jeanne-Marie and her granddaughter both beamed, and Vanessa smiled back, her momentary tension disappearing. "She's out of the hospital. We just had our engagement dinner last night."

"Congratulations! And I'm very glad she's all right. Was it coyotes? They've gotten so bold; I keep expecting to have to move my chickens all the way inside my house to keep those little bastards away!"

"Grandma," Henriette said, sounding more amused than exasperated. "She has other tables." She nodded across the way, to where Leanne Perkins was sitting alone, staring determinedly at the menu and tapping her foot.

"Oh, hush, I've known Leanne since she was in diapers and she could learn to practice some patience. I'll take the bleu cheese dressing, dear, and you tell Tiffany that Kendra's great-grandma says hello."

"I will."

~~*

"You sure you don't want me to bring your car around?"

Tiffany shook her head, giving John the best approximation of a smile that she could at the moment. It was her first night back at work, and he had insisted on showing up at the end of her shift and walking her to her car. She had insisted right back that it was unnecessary, that it had been a billion-to-one incident and she was fine now.

And she'd honestly believed that, right up until she'd walked out of the store and looked across the dark parking lot.

Move your feet, she told herself. Walk. Now.

"Tiffany," John said. "It's not a problem for me to—"

"No," she said. "I'm not some scared little kid."

"Nobody said that you were."

She took a deep breath, telling herself not to snap at him again. He was trying to help; it wasn't his fault that she was being chickenshit. "This isn't the last time I'm going to work night shift. You don't have to coddle me."

"Coddling would be me carrying you to your car," he pointed out. "This is just making sure you're safe. If it'll help you feel better, it's as much for Vanessa's sake as yours."

"…that does help, actually," she said. She took another deep breath. "Okay. Okay, let's go."

She forced her feet into motion, trying to ignore

how her heart started hammering in fear as she approached her parking space. John moved ahead of her, checking underneath and around her car.

"Nothing there," he said, and she felt such a rush of relief that she almost burst into tears.

And wouldn't *that* be embarrassing as all hell.

She unlocked her car. "John?"

"Yeah?"

Just say it, she thought. After all, he's pretty much going to be your father-in-law soon, and you don't want to have to call at one a.m. because you're frozen in the store doorway. "I've got night shift the next four nights. Would you mind, if…?"

"Tell me what time and I'll be here."

"Thanks," she said, once she was sure her voice wouldn't be wobbly when she spoke.   She sat down in her driver's seat and closed the door, trying not to remember how she'd run back toward the lights and safety of the store, how she hadn't made it, the small, sharp teeth punching through her skin.

Enough, she told herself. It was over and done with.

~~*

Sophia stared at the computer screen, and the words started to swim as her eyes filled with tears.

"Good news!" someone named Tanner Jefferson had posted. "Got one of the little bastards!"

A possum. He was bragging about how he'd shot a possum. He even gave the street where he'd done it.

Her thoughts swarmed around her head, fighting for dominance. She needed to tell her mom; she could go give this jerk a ticket or something for shooting a firearm in town. She needed to make her fingers work, needed to type a reply. Tell him that all he'd done was kill an innocent creature. Even Tiffany wasn't mad about what had happened to her. She knew it had been a fluke, and if the person who'd actually been hurt wasn't looking for revenge than he certainly had no right to.

He was just mean, she thought, wiping roughly at her eyes. Mean, and looking for an excuse to act out on it.

Then she looked at the timestamp on the post. Twenty-three minutes ago. And the address was less than three blocks away.

The least she could do was bury the poor thing.

The others were all in bed—she hadn't been able to get to sleep, and so had come out to the living room and turned on the computer—and her dad wouldn't be waking up to meet Tiffany at work for another hour and a half. Maybe she couldn't bury it in that length of time, but she could at least get it to their backyard and get most of the hole dug.

Feeling a little better now that she had a plan, had something to *do* rather than just sitting here and feeling helpless and angry, Sophia got up and headed into the kitchen, to the basket where her parents kept their cardboard for recycling.

She grabbed an Amazon box and then put on her shoes, getting her phone off the charger before she quietly left the house. Stopping at their little gardening shed, she dug around the supply boxes until she found her dad's thick leather gloves.

There hadn't been a picture, she told herself as she walked. Maybe Tanner had been lying, bragging about killing something so he could sound like a big man to his gross friends.

She really, really hoped he'd been lying.

Sophia looked around, picking up her pace. She wasn't a little kid anymore; she wasn't scared of the dark. But it was kinda creepy out here now that it was all shadowy and quiet and the streets were empty.

She reached the street Tanner had mentioned and looked around, for a moment seeing nothing out of the ordinary. Then she caught sight of a white lump in the ditch and sucked in a pained breath before running forward.

It was moving. It had dragged itself from the side of the road into the ditch. Now it lay still, taking shallow, ragged breaths.

Four babies were clinging to its back.

"You…you motherfucker," Sophia whispered. The word sounded strange on her lips, made her face turn red—unlike her friends, she wasn't much of a cusser—but it was either say a word that'd get her grounded for a month or just scream in grief and rage.

What did she do now? she wondered, watching the tiny animals crawl around on their dying mother's fur. She could call her boss, tell her it was an emergency, but it was kitten season. The shelter was already overwhelmed. As much as Mrs. Patton loved animals, she would likely advise euthanasia.

Couldn't be much different than caring for too-young kittens, she reasoned. Give them someplace warm, make sure they get milk.

Maybe they wouldn't make it, she thought. They were so small; had barely any fur on them and two of them didn't even have their eyes open yet. But she could at the very least give them a chance.

The mother gave a final, shuddering breath and then lay still.

"I'm sorry," Sophia whispered, wishing that she was a badass like her mom, that she carried a gun too so she could go to Tanner's house and make him go to jail, make him sit in a cell for weeks and weeks and *think* about taking a life for no reason.

That wasn't how the law worked, she told herself. She knew from eavesdropping on her mom and dad talking that it was hard enough to get people punished for deliberately abusing or neglecting their pets; the most this guy might get would be a fine for firing a gun within town limits.

Still.

"You'll be okay," she promised the babies, as she

put on the leather gloves. "I'll take care of you. You'll be okay."

Gingerly, she picked up each baby one by one, inspecting them to make sure that none of them had been winged by that jerk's bullet. Each of them had some blood on their fur, but it seemed to be their mother's.

She'd bathe them when she got home, she thought. Just get a damp washcloth, or maybe a baby wipe; she didn't want them to catch a chill.

Once the babies were all in the box, she started to turn away, and then she realized something.

Sophia groaned. Hadn't she just been talking to that lady on Facebook about the importance of doing this?

She had to check the pouch.

She set the box down and turned back to the body. The mother possum was lying on her side, and Sophia shone her phone flashlight all around, making sure again that no babies were lying in the grass. Once she knew the area was clear, she carefully knelt down next to the mother's body.
Turning her onto her back, mumbling a whispered apology, she carefully opened the pouch the way she'd watched on Youtube.

There were three more babies in there.

"Ohhh wow," she whispered, a little grossed out by the blood on her gloves—she'd have to use her allowance to buy her dad a new pair—but the awe overrode that. "Look at you."

One by one, she took hold of them as gently as she could. Detach them by holding the head, not the body, and pulling carefully but firmly; she'd read that. Her hands were clumsy in the big gloves, and she considered taking them off for this part, but in the end left them on. Possums didn't carry rabies, no, but they did carry other diseases. She would care for them, yes, but she shouldn't do it barehanded.

Soon the last three had joined their brothers and sisters in the box, and she breathed a sigh of relief. They were safe.

She'd transfer them into a smaller box—one with a soft, fluffy towel—and keep them under her bed. She needed to get a syringe to feed them with, and some baby kitten formula. That should be close enough to their mother's milk to hopefully keep them alive.

Or should she get cream, for extra nutrients?

That was baby bunnies, she thought. They got a little cream in with the kitten milk replacer. Maybe possums should, too?

She'd double-check. Some of their eyes were open; that meant they were around a couple of months old. Once they were settled in for the night, she'd read up on what she needed to do for them.

Sophia picked up the box, smiling down at her new charges as she carried them home.

~~*

"What in the fuck?" Tiffany whispered, staring at her reflection in the bathroom mirror.

The lightbulb over the mirror had gone out. She'd turned away, intent on getting a replacement from the kitchen, and she could've sworn her eyes had shone green in the meager light from the window.

She turned her head from side to side, nearly leaping back in fright when she saw it happen again.

Eyes were not supposed to do that.

She grabbed her phone, then slowly set it back down.

What was she supposed to say? "Hi, I think I've got eyeshine like a cat, which means I'm definitely hallucinating, so please run a whole bunch of expensive physical and mental tests"?

No. She was fine. She probably hadn't even seen eyeshine. Just some weird trick of the light, that was all. Plus, she was tired.

Against her will, her gaze fell to her legs.

She'd shaved yesterday, after realizing that her leg hair had turned bright white. It was starting to grow back.

Slowly, she removed her shirt and raised her arms, frowning at the snow-white fuzz under her arms.

Tiffany stripped off the rest of her clothes and climbed into the shower, first taking care of her calves again, and then shaving her bikini area and under her arms.

Stress reaction, she thought. Hadn't she heard those

old stories about people being scared so badly that their hair turned white?

The clinic had given her a clean bill of health. She was fine.

She was also still taking antibiotics. Maybe white hair was just a side effect from one of those.

That had to be it.

CHAPTER FIVE

"Hi, sweeties," Sophia whispered, taking out the shoebox she'd transferred them to after making sure that her door was locked.

One of them, the smallest, had died yesterday. But the others seemed to be doing fine.

She'd gone back yesterday night and gotten their mother, burying her in the backyard. Tonight, once everyone was asleep, she'd bury her baby with her.

Please, let that be the only one, she thought.

She'd thrown out her dad's bloody gloves and started using a pair of her mom's gardening gloves instead. They weren't as sturdy as the leather ones, but they were thick enough to protect against the babies' tiny teeth (not that any of them had shown the least bit of hostility) and it was much easier to maneuver her fingers in them.

One by one, she picked up the babies and carefully syringe-fed them. They made noises sometimes, not the high-pitched squeak of kittens, but a little sneezing sound. And once in a while, if she accidentally moved too quickly, one or two would hiss.

It was pretty much the cutest thing she'd ever seen, but she pretended to be intimidated nonetheless.

Once she was done feeding them, she stroked their tiny backs for a few moments, and then slid the shoebox back under her bed.

~~*

She buried the runt of the litter that night.

By the next morning's feeding, something had changed.

~~*

Sophia mixed their formula with a powdered calcium supplement, then pulled the shoebox out from under the bed.

The babies were crawling around, but there was something…off about it. They were moving a little too fast, and their mouths were all open, panting and hissing.

"Oh no," she whispered. Were they sick?

"Sophia?" her mother called, rapping on her door. "Come on. Let's go to Walmart; I want to pick you up a new pair of sandals. Yours are falling apart."

"Just a sec!" she called. She fed the babies about every three hours; they'd be super-hungry by the time she got back. Her mom's 'just one thing' trips tended to turn into 'just twenty things'.

She picked up a tiny decorative plate from her bookshelf, pouring some formula into it and placing it in the shoebox before sliding it back under the bed. Some of the babies were lapping their food up that way and this would tide most of them over; she'd make sure everyone had gotten enough food as soon as she got back.

"Why was your door locked?" her mom asked, as she stepped out into the hall.

"I was writing in my diary," Sophia lied, a little ashamed by how easily the words came out.

Well, it wasn't like she was lying so she could go party with friends or something. This was important.

Her mom gave her a puzzled look, but Sophia could see the exact instant she thought, "Well, teenagers" and decided to change the subject. "You need new tennis shoes, too, or just sandals?"

She could use both, but it could wait. She wanted to get back as soon as possible. "Just sandals."

An hour and a half, ten pairs of tried-on shoes, two bags of groceries, and one "grumping fit" (as her mom called it) later, they left the store.

When they were a couple of blocks away from their house, her mom's phone rang. She pulled over to answer it, and Sophia bit back a groan.

"Hey, Ness," her mom said. "What's wrong?"

She listened for a few minutes and then ended the call, setting the phone back in the cupholder between their seats. "I'm going to run by Tiffany's. She called in sick to work, and told Ness not to come by. Said she's got the flu; I want to make sure she doesn't need to go to the doctor."

"Can you drop me at home first?"

Her mom gave her a look, and she smiled apologetically. "Sorry?" She lowered her voice. "I've got cramps something awful, mom, I really just want to lie down."

That first part, at least, wasn't another lie.

"Why didn't you say something?" her mom said, voice and look sympathetic now. "We could've gotten your shoes tomorrow."

"I was hoping they'd fade off."

"Not with my genes," her mom said. "Sorry, kiddo." She drove to their house and pulled into the driveway. "Remember—"

"Ibuprofen and a heating pad. I know."

"And take the groceries in, would you? Ask your dad to put them away."

"I will."

Sophia left the groceries and the box containing her new shoes on the kitchen table, called to her dad, and then hurried back into her room.

She closed the door and locked it and put on her gloves, then pulled the shoebox out from under the bed.

None of them would eat. They just hissed at her, flailing their tiny bodies back and forth in her hands, thin tails whapping ineffectually against her wrists.

Something was really wrong.

She put them all back into the shoebox and set it on the floor, taking out her phone and opening one of the possum-care websites she'd found. She didn't remember ever reading about anything like this.

Then she felt something on her foot and looked

down.

The babies had tipped over the shoebox and were now scurrying around on the carpet, moving much faster than they should be able to. One of them was on her now-bare foot, hissing up at her.

Yelping in surprise, she tilted her foot and dumped the tiny animal off. At the sound, the others turned to her simultaneously, changing direction to run at her feet.

She shrieked and jumped up onto the bed.

"Sophia?" her dad called from the kitchen. "Everything okay?"

"Yeah, yeah!" she said, staring down at the snarling babies. "Everything's fine! Just saw a spider, that's all!"

"You sure?" he asked. Right outside her door now.

"Yep! I'm good!"

He was silent for a few seconds, and then tried the door. "Let me in, please."

"Not, um…not a good time. I'm fine. I promise."

"Sophia. What's the matter?"

What was she supposed to say? "Nothing!"

"Open this door, young lady."

She glared at the door, a retort on her lips, but then she looked down again and saw that the three largest babies were climbing the bedspread.

It shouldn't be scary. Only little kids would think it was scary; the babies were only about six inches long.

But the sight of them with their eyes locked on her, growling, had her screaming again.

"Daddy!"

A few seconds later he kicked the door in, taking in the scene around him with open-mouthed shock. Then one of the babies turned from her and scurried toward him, and he raised his foot.

"No!" she cried. "They're sick! They're just sick! Don't!"

"Did one of them bite you?"

"No, no, they tried but I always wear gloves. I'm not stupid!"

"I know that, but *this* wasn't smart! Come on," he said, holding out his arms as the largest of the babies made it up to the top of the bed. "Jump."

She leaped from the bed and he caught her, pulling the broken door as close to in-place as it would go. "Get some towels from the bathroom; we'll block this gap."

Sophia did so, and he pushed towels into the new space at the bottom of the broken door.   "If they've got whatever's going around," he said, "the clinic might be able to—"

"No! They'll kill them to study them!"

"You saw what happened to Tiffany," he said. "That can't happen to anybody else."

"I know. But I can get you a different one!"

"What?"

"Their mom! This jerk on Facebook shot their poor mom and bragged about it, and I found where she crawled off to die."

He crossed his arms, staring down at her. "When was this?"

"Dad, c'mon, please, can you ground me later?"

"I absolutely will." He sighed. "Where?"

~~*

Rebecca Navarro pulled into Tiffany's driveway and parked, striding up to the front door. She hoped that her niece's girlfriend—fiancee, she reminded herself—really did just have something that could be fixed with over-the-counter medicine. She didn't relish the idea of flat-out dragging her to the clinic, but she would if she had to.

She'd gone over their finances again last night, in anticipation of whatever charges from Tiffany's overnight stay might be left once financial aid covered some arbitrary amount.

It wasn't a lot, but better than nothing. And her grandmother (bless her departed soul) had been in love with bonds ever since she'd helped sell them during WWII, and had bought one for Rebecca every year on her birthday, and then for Sophia as well, until she'd passed away just before Sophia had turned four. If financial aid didn't cover much, she could cash some of those.

She'd intended to cash all of them once Sophia turned 18, as a gift to her daughter, but she'd already had to cash some when Vanessa had suddenly needed to move in. Her child's only hope at college was a very good scholarship, but she'd hoped to be able to give her a bit more in order to get started, should she choose to go.

Well. Life happened.

She rapped on the door, and heard a hoarse, "Go away."

Rebecca frowned. Vanessa had been right; Tiffany's voice did sound strange. She must have one hell of a sore throat; even if she didn't need to go to the clinic she'd at least run by the store and get her some cough medicine and a few bags of lozenges.

"Tiffany?" she called. "It's Becca. I need to come in."

"No."

"That wasn't a request," Becca said. She wasn't using her Cop Voice, but according to Vanessa, her Mom Voice was even more no-nonsense. "I need to see how you're doing, and whether or not you need to see a doctor."

"No doctors!" she exclaimed, and it sounded like a rough snarl.

"I know you're worried about the money," Becca said, gentling her tone. "And believe me, I know how hard it is to ask for help. But you're family. We'll take care of you. If you have to go back to the clinic, I will set up a payment plan for you so you can pay us back if it'll make you feel better. I promise we won't charge interest."

She got an approximation of a laugh at that, but it was raspy and pained.

Enough of this, she thought, taking a hairpin out of

her bun. She would make amends with Tiffany however she needed to later. Right now the girl was hurting.

She picked the lock—it was far too easy to do; she'd have a talk with Tiffany's landlord about providing better security—and opened the door.

Tiffany was curled on the couch, buried in blankets, and she wailed at the sight of Rebecca coming into the house. "No! I told you I'm fine!"

"You don't sound fine. Come on. What are your symptoms?" she asked, stopping about ten feet away from the couch.

"I…I can't."

"Tiffany," she said. "I've been a mom for over a decade. I promise you, I have heard, seen, and cleaned up after it all. I won't say a word to anyone besides the doctor, if you need one. But I have to know what's going on here."

Tiffany must have realized from her tone that she would march over there and pull the blanket away if need be, because she finally, slowly, lowered the thick flannel.

"Oh my god," Rebecca breathed.

Tiffany's eyes had gone entirely black. Fur covered her skin, white on her face and grayish-white further down her body. As she stared, Tiffany let out a sob that sounded more like a hiss, exposing wickedly pointed teeth.

"I told you to go away," Tiffany cried. "I can't go to a doctor. I can't. They'll…they'll lock me up and never let me out."

Rebecca closed the distance between them,

crouching down so that they were eye-to-eye. Whatever was happening, this was Tiffany. "Hey," she said. "You know me. Do you trust me?"

"Yes."

"Then trust that I will not let that happen. John and Ness and I will be with you every step of—"

"No! You can't tell Ness. You can't."

"Then John or I will be there," Rebecca amended. "I don't know what the hell's going on, but I do know you can't hunker down in here hoping that it'll get better. Come on," she said, wrapping the blanket around her again so that it draped over her face. "Out to the car. I'll get you to the clinic."

Tiffany nodded, sniffling miserably, and followed her outside. Rebecca opened the passenger side door for her and she awkwardly climbed in, trying to use the blanket to cover every inch possible. "I'm sorry," she whispered, a moment or two later.

"Nothing to be sorry about."

"I knew a couple of days ago that something was going on. But I didn't say anything. I thought it'd go away."

"Wouldn't be the first time someone's done that," Rebecca said, as she waited at the four-way stop for her turn and then pulled out onto Main Street. "John used to work out at the sawmill; there were a couple of days when he was dead on his feet and still wanted to pretend he could work a full day just fine. And he calls me stubborn."

Tiffany groaned, a pained sound to it that she recognized all too well. "If you need to throw up, I'll pull over."

Tiffany shook her head, then groaned again, and Rebecca sped up slightly as she turned onto the road approaching the clinic. "We'll be there in just a minute or two, sweetheart. You'll be fine."

She glanced over at her just as Tiffany threw the blanket off, teeth bared and black eyes wide with fury, and lunged.

CHAPTER SIX

"Hey, Danny," John said, keeping an eye on Sophia's door. "Strange question—you still have that old aquarium?"

"Yeah," Danny Stewart said. "Shows me not to go to one of those fancy pet stores ever again. Y'know, the goldfish died in that pricey thing just as sure as they died in a simple glass bowl. Why d'you ask?"

"I was wondering if I could borrow it for a few days."

"Sure, yeah. Want me to run it by tonight before work?"

"Think I'm gonna need it a bit sooner than that."

Danny laughed. "What'd that little girl of yours bring home now?"

"You don't want to know," John said, and Sophia was relieved to see that the smile that crossed his face, while brief, did seem genuine.

She rubbed one bare foot across the top of the other, scratching a sudden itch. Stupid mosquitoes.

"Come on," her dad said, putting his cell phone back into his pocket. "We're going to the Stewart's house."

"Maybe I should stay here," she said. "What if they get out?"

"That's exactly why you should not stay here," he said. He looked around the living room, then motioned to one of the bookcases. "Here, help me slide this."

They did, pushing it across the floor until it was in front of her door. "There. Now, if that doesn't do it—what's the only way to be sure?"

"Nuke the site from orbit," she recited, smiling. Though she hadn't been allowed to see Aliens until last year, she'd known the quote all her life—her dad said it pretty much anytime he saw a spider.

They drove to the Stewart's house and Danny answered the door. He was a heavyset man with a contagious smile and a penchant for practical jokes. His five kids were daredevils to the last, but none of them were mean about it. Sophia went to school with his son Tim, who in kindergarten had kicked Jimmy Hauptman in the nuts when he'd asked to see the slug she was carrying outside to safety and then dumped a packet of salt from the cafeteria on it.
Tim had gotten suspended for three days, but she knew his mom had brought home an ice cream sundae for him (she'd said as much when Sophia had dropped off her thank-you note).

"Hey, Soph," Danny said now, grinning and reaching down to ruffle her hair. "So is it a snapping turtle?"

"No," she said. "Baby possums."

Danny paused as he went inside to get the aquarium. "You sure that's a good idea?" he asked. "Heard those things have been gettin' kinda nasty lately."

"They're just babies," she protested. "And besides, if they do get nasty, it just means they're sick and need a vet, not that they shouldn't be helped!"

"Whoa, whoa," he said. "Easy there, Steve Irwin. Of course you should help them. Just be careful, huh?"

"I always am," she said, rubbing at the top of her foot with the bottom of her new sandal. Then she looked down and frowned. The welt was bigger than she'd expect with a mosquito. Spider bite?

As her father took the aquarium and said his goodbyes to Danny, she walked out to the car silently, another thought having struck.

The baby possum had been on her foot. And no, it hadn't bitten her, but what if one of its tiny claws had scratched her foot when she'd dumped it off? She hadn't felt anything, but if it had been a little enough scrape…

"You okay?" her father asked, after they were back home and had moved the bookshelf back to its proper place. While he'd gingerly gathered the babies—wearing the thickest pair of gloves he'd been able to find in the shed—she'd mixed up a good-sized plate of formula and put it in the aquarium first, so they wouldn't have to be hand-fed until they figured out what was wrong. "You've been awfully quiet."

"Just worried about the babies," she said. "I'll feel a lot better once they're okay."

"I hope they'll be okay, too, but you know we can't promise anything," he said, eyeing a few of the heavier books before he placed them on top of the mesh aquarium lid for good measure.

The babies were still hissing—when she moved her finger in front of one of them it threw itself at the glass, open-mouthed, trying in vain to snap at her. "This really isn't right," she whispered. "We should take them to the vet."

"It's Sunday," he pointed out. "You'll have to call Mrs. Patton."

"Okay." She started to tug her cell phone out of her shorts pocket, and then winced as the itch on her foot seemed to triple. And not just itching now, it *burned*.

What are you going to do? she thought. Be the creep in the horror movie who doesn't say anything about being bitten by a zombie until it's too late?

"Dad?" she muttered, resisting the urge to stare at the floor. "I…I think maybe I wasn't being as smart as I thought."

His gaze sharpened. "What do you mean?"

"Here, look," she said, taking off her sandal to reveal the red welt. She nearly gaped at it herself; it had almost tripled in size since she'd put the shoe on. "One of the babies crawled onto my foot. I dumped it right off; I didn't realize it had scratched me until we were at Mr. Stewart's house, dad, I promise."

"Come on."

He grabbed her hand and they hurried to the car, barely pausing to lock the front door behind them. "What about the babies?" Sophia cried.

"I'll call your mom and tell her to take them to Mrs. Patton. Right now, you're going to the clinic."

She dug her heels in, trying to skid to a stop as he opened the passenger side door for her. "Am I gonna have to get a shot?"

He hesitated. The question was a lot bigger, he knew, than her phobia of needles. The welt on her foot already had a black ring around it. He never thought he'd hope for a brown recluse bite, but at the moment it was actually the better case scenario. "I don't know," he said. "But we can't just leave it like that."

"But why is it happening so quickly?" she asked, reluctantly getting into the car. She'd left her other sandal off in deference to the wound. "Tiffany got bitten and scratched; this didn't happen to her!"

"Maybe it would have if she hadn't gotten to the clinic so fast."

"Yeah, maybe. Does that mean I have to get an IV?"

"You'll get whatever the doctor says you need, and once you're back home, you can watch any movie you want."

She brightened. "*Anything*?"

"Your choice."

"Even if I want to marathon all the Saw movies?"

He glanced sideways at her. "I would hope you'd have better taste, but yes, even those."

"Or maybe I'll watch Jaws!"

"That's a good pick. There are a kid and a dog who don't make it out, though. Fair warning."

Sophia's eyes widened. "A kid *and* a dog? And they did that in the sixties?"

"Seventies," he corrected. "And just because some horror movies were made before you were born doesn't mean they're tame. Texas Chainsaw Massacre still gives me nightmares."

She grinned. "Really?"

"You are *not* watching—"

"You said anything," she said, before she winced and leaned down to rub at her foot.

"You okay?" he asked. She nodded, though the grimace on her face said otherwise. "Try not to touch it."

"But it itches," she complained. "It's—"

Then her dad hit the brakes hard enough that she bumped her head on the dashboard, given that she was leaning over. "What?" she asked, pressing a hand to her head as she sat up. "Is—" Then she screamed. A familiar car was off the road, its hood crunched in from a head-on collision with an enormous sycamore. "*Mom*!"

Before her father could tell her to stay in the car, she was unfastening her seatbelt with shaking hands and scrambling out, racing toward the wrecked police cruiser before her dad caught hold of her and pulled her back.

"Stay here," he said, and she'd never heard him sound that grim, that empty.

It was because her mom might still be in the car, she thought frantically. Hurt or…or worse and he didn't want her to see.

"Rebecca?"

"Mom!" she yelled. No answer. "Mom, say something!"

"She's not in the car," her dad said, once he'd moved close enough to check. "It's okay. You know how she brakes for everything, right?" He glanced back, gave her a reassuring smile before giving the car another once-over and returning to her side. "I'm sure that's what happened. Squirrel ran out in front of her, she hit the brakes and lost control. It happens. Radio looks like it got busted in the crash, so she would've just walked to the clinic."

"Okay," she sniffled. Parts of that didn't sound right to her—her mom was one of the best drivers she knew; surely a squirrel wouldn't make her crash, especially if there wasn't black ice or something. Just a straight, dry stretch of road. And maybe the radio was busted, but her cell phone probably wasn't. The clinic phones definitely wouldn't be. Why hadn't she called?

But her dad wasn't panicking, which meant he didn't want her to panic either. And she wouldn't. Even if it did feel like she was about to throw up.

Then she heard a rustling noise from the other side of the car, off in the trees. "Mom?" What if she'd gotten disoriented and headed into the woods instead of onto the road?

The creature that stepped out had two familiar features—Tiffany's short natural curls, and the 25-cent ring that Vanessa had gotten her at one of the vending machines at Carlota's as a placeholder until they could buy real ones. But now her hair was streaked with gray, and the ring was wrapped around a finger that ended in a wicked claw. Gone, too, was her black skin; it was covered entirely in gray-white fur.

She stared at what had become of Tiffany, almost in a trance, unable to move even when her sister's fiancee opened her mouth to bare dozens of needle-sharp teeth.

"Holy shit," she breathed, and the bone-deep Child Knowledge of "a parent just heard me cuss and now I'm gonna get it" snapped her out of it enough to retreat. Then her dad moved her behind him.

"Tiffany?" he asked softly.

A low growl was his only answer.

"Sophia. I want you to move, very slowly, back toward the car."

"What about you?"

"Do what I say."

She carefully retreated, glancing back every once in a while to make sure she wasn't about to trip over a branch or step in a hole.

Then she doubled over, groaning in pain as a bolt of agony flared from her foot straight up to her stomach.

"Sophia?" her father asked, not daring to look away from Tiffany, whose black eyes were locked on him. "Are you okay?"

"It hurts," she gasped.

"Sophia?" another voice called, and despite the pain, she looked up to see her mother, leaning against a tree near her wrecked car. Her forehead had a cut across it and her face was bloody, and her left arm was dangling at an odd angle, but she was standing. She was okay.

"Mom!"

And if she'd thought the baby possums moved fast, that was nothing compared to how quickly Tiffany moved now, darting around her father and grabbing her by the arms hard, claws digging into her skin. She yelped in pain and both her parents ran toward her—though her mother's was more an awkward stumble than a run—but then Tiffany froze, loosening her hold. She tilted her head, teeth no longer on display, looking more questioning than hostile.

"Mom, dad, stop!" Sophia ordered. She felt like she was teetering on the edge of a cliff, and that the wrong move would send her over the edge instead of bringing her to safety. "It's okay, Tiffany," she whispered. "It's me. It's Sophia. You remember me, right? I'm Vanessa's cousin. I know you remember Vanessa."

Tiffany sniffed at her hair with her slightly elongated nose, making an odd chuffing noise.

The pain arced through her again, even stronger this time, and as white hair began to sprout thickly from her arms, she realized why Tiffany hadn't bitten her.

There was no need. Like had called to like.

Her nose felt like it was breaking from the inside out, and she clutched at her face. She heard footsteps coming closer and Tiffany growled again, starting to turn away from her.

"Dad, run. Get mom," she gasped. "Run."

"We're not—"

"Please!"

She looked up at him, wondering dimly if her eyes were turning black, too, and then even that wayward thought was subsumed by a wave of anger, irrational and overwhelming, telling her to bare her teeth, to charge, to bite…

No!

She whimpered, clutching at Tiffany's sleeve, unsure whether she was seeking comfort or trying to hold her back from doing the exact same thing she was suddenly so driven to do.

Sophia saw the moment the truth registered on her dad's face. If she did get violent, if she went for him or her mother, there was no way either of them would be able to hurt her. They'd all be lost.

Wrapping her arms around Tiffany, she was surprised when Tiffany hugged her in return. Was it because some part of her still remained human, or because whatever had taken her over felt maternal toward a smaller one of its own kind?

She saw her father reach her mother, saw him lift

her into his arms, and decided it didn't matter what Tiffany's motives were. As long as her parents reached that car, as long as they got away, then they would figure out a plan. They would come back for her.

The pain washed through her again, and she started to sink to the ground, but Tiffany made that same sound again, more comforting than questioning this time, and tugged her toward the trees. She reluctantly kept pace, feeling better once she kicked off her remaining sandal. The bare earth felt wonderful against her feet, soothing some of the pain, and as they went deeper into the forest she heard a sound, something oddly familiar

(car engine)

Engine? she thought, trying to puzzle out the strange word.

Then her friend tightened her grip on her hand, and she looked ahead, smiling. There was no need to wonder what en…whatever that word had been meant. Her friend would guide her. Would take her to food, to water.

To prey.

~~*

Leader led Apprentice deeper into the woods, smiling in pride as they came closer to the clearing where she'd instructed their smaller brethren to wait.

Before she had come along, they had been scattered, disorganized. They had taken blood for their Father, yes, but it had been haphazard, and some of her little cousins been killed as well.

Now she was here for them, and she had helped young Apprentice go through her change faster. Following their instruction, the cousins would be much more effective hunters.

She didn't know what Father looked like, what his voice sounded like, but she felt his presence in her head, instructing her, ordering her to find unmarked flesh and tear it open.

Every human—bringers of death that they were, with their giant rumbling machines that attacked when they crossed the smooth black paths and the deafening weapons that murdered even at a distance—would fertilize the ground, would rot and draw forth the bugs that their little cousins would so enjoy.

Before, all they had done against the onslaught of humans was hiss. Or worse, they would lie very still and hope mercy would be shown, that they would be allowed to waddle back into the woods to their dens, to their babies.

They would now show as much mercy as they'd been shown. Father had given them the instinct, the drive, the permission.

Apprentice let out a startled hiss as they reached the clearing, and Leader beamed, regarding her cousins. They numbered in the hundreds. Some were old, barely able to walk under their own power anymore, but she knew that when the time came they would fight regardless. So would the mothers with the babies still in pouches, or clinging to their backs.

She wrapped an arm around Apprentice's shoulders, reassuring her as they moved fully into the clearing. The little cousins moved to make a path for them and then closed ranks, leaving them completely surrounded.

Leader closed her eyes tightly, thinking of the images, the smells, of places in town that Father had given to her. And people, all the people. There was one in particular, the picture of her dark, wrinkled face as clear as spring water, to save for last. But the rest…

She concentrated on those images, sending them first to Apprentice, and then both of them working together to send them to the little cousins.

Gently, she admonished Apprentice, when the younger female began to broadcast images with all her strength. *Their minds are so much smaller than ours.*

Apprentice nodded and then slammed her eyes shut again, helping her to pass on the messages, but carefully this time.

The cousins grew more and more agitated, their thoughts filling with the idea of using their teeth, of drawing blood.

Leader stepped forward, knowing the smaller ones would move. They did, making way for her and Apprentice again, hissing and snarling.

They were ready now. It was time.

Once she and Apprentice were through the crowd,

the swarm followed.

CHAPTER SEVEN

"You drop me off," Becca said, sounding remarkably stern for someone nursing a broken arm and a likely concussion. "You drop me off, and then you go back out and get Sophia. Or at least…at least make sure she's somewhere safe. The basement," she said. "I think we have a couple of deadbolts in the garage. Put them on the outside of our basement door. If you can get her down there…maybe she'll still recognize you. Or you can use food as a lure? What do possums eat, I know Sophia's told me…"

She was sounding more and more dazed with each word, and John kept one hand on the steering wheel, using the other to stroke carefully through her hair. "I'll make sure she's safe. I promise."

"I know."

She closed her eyes, leaning into his hand as he parked in front of the clinic. She remained still, too still, for a few seconds, and then she opened her eyes again and reached for the door handle, no more pain visible on her face, her expression schooled fully into "I will take no shit today".

Smiling briefly, he got out and walked with her to the door, helping to support her weight as much as she would allow (which wasn't much).

"I had a wreck," Becca announced to the surprised

receptionist. "I need this arm set, and probably some stitches up here," she said, motioning to her blood-crusted forehead with her good hand. "And painkillers, but nothing that'll put me out."

"Y…yes, Chief," the receptionist said, picking up the phone to contact the doctor. She frowned, staring at the receiver. "That's odd. No dial tone. I'll go get him," she said, standing up from her desk and hurrying down the hall.

John took his cell phone out of his pocket. The little 4G symbol was gone, not even a 1G or a local WiFi option in its place.

The screech of brakes had them both turning in time to see a battered pickup truck nearly rear-end John's car. An elderly black woman climbed out, leaning hard on her cane.

John frowned. Jeanne-Marie Broussard lived on the outskirts of town and was a fixture at the local farmer's market. Tiffany worked with her great-grandaughter. Kayla? No, Kendra.

But the last time he'd seen her, Jeanne-Marie had gotten around better at 94 than a lot of people did at 70. Now she gripped her cane like it was a lifeline, and she seemed to have lost weight.

"Chief!" she cried, as soon as she came into the building. "Thank God you're here. Something awful's happening, and—" She paused, looking Becca over. "Maybe you already know that."

"I do indeed," Becca muttered. "What's wrong,

Jeanne-Marie? Were you bitten? Scratched?”

“No. But I think I know why this is happening.”

Becca’s eyes lit with interest, but then the receptionist came hurrying in with Dr. Whittaker (the receptionist was, fortunately, pushing a wheelchair—Becca didn’t look like she’d be able to walk under her own power for much longer).

It was testament to how much she was hurting that she sat down in the wheelchair instead of protesting that she didn’t need it. John knelt in front of her.

“Vanessa should still be at the diner. The two of us’ll be able to get Sophia somewhere safe. Okay?”

She nodded, clutching his hands with her good one before leaning across to give him a brief kiss.

“Jeanne-Marie?” she said, as John reluctantly got to his feet. “You want to come back with me, tell me what’s going on?”

The older woman shook her head. “I’ll go with him,” she said. “I need to check on my family, too.”

~~*

Instead of talking, Jeanne-Marie rode in silence, staring out the window and chewing on her bottom lip almost hard enough to draw blood.

“What happened to your leg?” John asked, by way of getting a conversation started. “Saw you last weekend at the farmer’s market, you were—”

"Diabetes," she said. "Doc said they might have to take part of my left leg."

He blinked. "It can come on that fast?"

"Not in my case. Not without help. I think—I *know*—my brother cursed me."

John gave her a quick glance. Her twin, Baptiste, was a cantankerous asshole, but a *curse*? "Jeanne-Marie…"

"Hush. I said I'd tell you what happened, not that you'd have to believe me. Watch out!" she said, and he hit the brakes as over a dozen possums charged across the road. "Sorry," she said. "Honestly, you should've run over as many as you could, but old habits."

"I know," he said, slowing down as he regarded the animals' destination: Burke Wireless, the town's internet provider.

Damn things probably chewed through all the wiring, he thought. He hoped the employees were all right. He'd check, as soon as he'd gotten Vanessa and Sophia to safety.

He pulled to a stop in front of the Sunny Side Up Diner. "Wait here," he told Jeanne-Marie.

In response, she held out her cane. "Take this."

He started to ask why, and then saw the large possum crouching by the front door. It almost looked like it was standing guard.

No, couldn't be. They weren't that smart, were they?

But then, they also weren't supposed to attack

people.

He took Jeanne-Marie's cane and shut the car door, then turned on the growling animal. He poked at it with the cane, trying to convince it to go somewhere else. It hissed.

Then he heard a scream from inside the diner.

Shit.

"Sorry, Sophia," he whispered. He couldn't risk getting bitten, and he didn't have time to try and nudge or lure this thing away.

He brought the cane down hard.

~~*

"Ness. If you're not going to pay attention, you need to go home. That's the third order you've messed up this morning."

Vanessa sighed. Normally she might try to defend herself—anyone who worked as waitstaff had an off day once in a while—but her boss was right. "Sorry, Mrs. Hernandez," she said. "I'm just worried about Tiffany. I asked Aunt Becca to call as soon as she checked on her, and it's been over an hour. I tried calling them, but neither of them answered, and…"

Mrs. Hernandez's expression softened a little, and she rested a hand on her shoulder. "Tell you what. Once the church crowd's done with their lunch, you go ahead and take the rest of the afternoon off. We can handle it from there."

"Thanks so much."

"And remember, your aunt probably just got a call-out for more graffiti on the old Bryant place or something. And you said Tiffany wasn't feeling well. I bet she's taking a nap."

"I know," Vanessa said. "I just worry."

Her boss smiled. "You take after John. Now, go on to Table 4, all right?"

"Got it."

She started over to Table 4—which was, blessedly, an easy enough table. Mr. Sharma and his son came in every Sunday at the same time, always ordering ice waters, while Mr. Sharma got the #8 lunch special and his son got the #3.

Then she heard a shriek from the back of the diner, and turned.

Madison, their dishwasher, came charging around the back counter, taking gasping breaths. She looked near tears. "I was taking the trash out and this thing *bit* me!" she wailed, tugging down her knee-high uniform sock to display a bloody mark.

"What was it?" Mrs. Hernandez asked, kneeling down to take a closer look.

Vanessa retreated a step. She had a sick feeling that she already knew that answer. "Did you shut the door?"

"What?" Madison asked, sniffling as she stared down at her leg.

"When you ran back inside, did you shut the door

behind you?"

"I don't—" she began, but then they all got the answer when about fifteen possums charged around the counter, teeth bared, hissing at the customers.

Several of them shouted in alarm, with many climbing right up onto the tables. Madison made for the door, just as someone outside opened it.

"Uncle John!" Vanessa called. "What are you—"

Doing here, she almost finished, but then she saw the Lawson family. The parents and Tyler, their eight-year old, were standing on their table, and Debra Lawson had lifted their baby's highchair entirely rather than waste time trying to unbuckle him.

Several possums had focused in on them, given the baby's wailing. They were climbing the sides of the vinyl-covered booth, snarling. Tyler—whom she'd known since he'd been the baby in the highchair—was shrieking, tears streaming down his face as he clung to his mother's leg.

She turned, grabbing hold of one of the serving trays they kept to-go boxes and cups on. She swung it at the possum that had gotten closest to the Lawsons. The animal slammed into the nearby counter and lay still. She doubted it was dead, but at least it wasn't actively attacking. She hit another one, and then her uncle was next to her, knocking the next one away with a cane.

Where had he gotten a cane?

Not really important, she thought, giving a fierce kick to a possum that went for her leg. All of the other customers had run out of the diner, though Mrs. Hernandez had stayed, and was currently hitting wayward possums with one of the stools.

Now that the possums weren't so close anymore, Debra set the highchair down on the table and unbuckled her son, holding him close in one arm, her free hand on her older son's back.

Keith Lawson—who worked at the local water plant and therefore had to wear steel-toed boots to be around the machinery—put one of those boots to good use by kicking a nearby possum halfway across the diner before stepping down off the table. He helped Debra down, then picked up Tyler, and they ran for the door.

"Oh my god," Debra cried.

At least a hundred possums were running down the street, several splitting off from the larger pack to run into backyards or squeeze themselves through a cat or dog door to get into houses.

"Can you get to your car?" John asked.

Debra shook her head, pointing down the street to where it was parked about a block and a half away. "I don't think so, no."

"The basement," Mrs. Hernandez said. "You can hide down there."

"What about you?" Keith asked.

"I'm getting to my car," she said. "My husband might need help." She nodded toward the basement door.

Neither of the Lawson adults bothered to ask if they

could go with her—she drove a four-seat pickup, and there was no car seat. They hurried to the basement door, Debra preceding the others down.

"John? Vanessa?" Keith asked, as his older son clattered down the stairs.

John shook his head. "Go on."

Keith nodded, and shut the door behind him.

As he did so, Mrs. Hernandez ran back to the kitchen and grabbed a cast iron skillet, holding it in one hand as she snatched the fire extinguisher off the wall. "Pin," she said.

Vanessa pulled it for her, and Mrs. Hernandez marched outside, spraying every possum she saw with the cold foam. She cleared a safe path to John's vehicle and then ran to her own, smacking hissing animals away with the skillet when the fire extinguisher ran out.

Vanessa clambered into the backseat, looking startled to see Jeanne-Marie in the passenger side. John got into the driver's seat and handed her cane back and then shut them safely in the car, waiting for Mrs. Hernandez to get into her truck before starting the engine.

"Where are we going?" Vanessa asked. "Where's Sophia? Is she with Aunt Becca? Did she go check on Tiffany; is she okay? We need to—"

"Your aunt's at the hospital," he said. "She's okay, just got a little banged up when her car went off the road. Tiffany and Sophia…"

"What?" When he didn't immediately answer, panic

flared in her eyes. "Oh my god. Are they—?"

"No, no!" he exclaimed. "I just didn't know how to…they've *changed*."

"Changed how?"

CHAPTER EIGHT

Alexis stared at her reflection in the mirror, watching the way her expression tightened when Dylan let out his obnoxious cackle of a laugh from the main room. She raised the joint to her lips, blowing the smoke out the open bathroom window. If she smoked out there, Caleb's dipshit friends would complain until she shared.

They could smoke their own cheap-ass pot. She didn't spend her money on the good stuff so they could use it all.

So here she was, hiding in the bathroom of her own place for some peace and quiet.

Caleb hadn't told her they were coming over today. Used to be, he was a lot better about that.

Used to be, a lot of things were different.

She sighed, closing her eyes. She'd started dating Caleb when they were both freshmen, and had gotten engaged senior year. Now, nearly a decade out of high school, there still wasn't an actual wedding ring on her finger and their plan of moving to Kansas City or Wichita had fizzled like so many other things.

Like the house they were going to buy together. She'd gotten and kept a job, and for six years out of high school he had, too. Then Dylan had moved back to town (fired from his office job after 'problems with some HR bitch', as had Andy (parents finally cut him off after he'd missed most of his classes at Pittsburg State University due to hangovers).

Just like that, the old gang had been back together, and what had been gatherings every two weeks or so had turned into every week, and then every Friday and Saturday.

Two years ago, Caleb had been late to work one too many times and lost his job. They'd lost their small house when he hadn't found another job in time and her paycheck hadn't been enough to make payments and utilities.

He'd fallen into a depression then, and stopped looking for work for a while. And she didn't blame him for that; she really didn't. It had knocked her on her ass, too. She just wished he'd come to her for comfort, rather than bouncing back and forth between his friends' places.

When she'd gotten a second job, she'd issued him an ultimatum: if he didn't get a job right away, fine. She knew opportunities could be few and far between. But he was at least going to be there for her when she got back to the mobile home she was renting, and stop spending every spare minute with his friends drinking beer they couldn't afford.

And he hadn't gotten mad, like she'd feared. He'd agreed that he'd been unfair to her, and for almost a year and a half it had been nice. They'd put wedding talk on the back burner until both of them could find better-paying jobs and get back into an actual house again ("I don't mind trailer parks," she'd told him. "I grew up in one. But I don't want to raise a kid in one, not in Tornado Alley."). But he had been home every night, dinner on the table, their home clean and neat and his breath not smelling like cheap beer.

Then Trevor had started coming over. And she didn't mind Trevor; he was quiet and polite and generally kept to himself. But then Andy had started coming over with Trevor, and Andy always brought booze.

And where there was booze, the others followed, and eventually she'd come home from work to find herself in a space that didn't feel at all like hers anymore.

So she'd talked to Caleb again. No ultimatums this time (though there had been, she hated to admit, some tears. Being an angry crier sucked).

He'd promised to do better. Cut things back to a poker game once every two weeks.
But now he was slipping again.

Alexis blew more smoke out the window, wishing she could blame her reddened eyes solely on the pot. She sniffled, brushing tears away.

She'd initially thought that Trevor's girlfriend Sam was being a bitch when she'd walked out and apparently never looked back, but maybe she'd just been smart. What if she herself had been brave enough to call Dylan or some of the other assholes out on their bullshit years ago? What if she hadn't made excuse after excuse for Caleb?

"Hey Lexi!" Andy said from outside the door. "You gonna be in there all day? I gotta take a piss!"

"Shut the fuck up, bro," she heard Caleb call. "Go

outside if you gotta go that bad. It's her bathroom."

He was, technically, sticking up for her. Once upon a time it would've made her smile. Now she wondered why he didn't just throw all of them out. How many times had she told him that she didn't want them there so much? He had to have realized that she fled for the bathroom more often than not as soon as more than two of them showed up at a time. She didn't want to be one of those brats who told their boyfriend that he couldn't hang around his friends, but…

God, she was tired.

The joint done, Alexis waved more air outside, then spritzed on some perfume to cover the scent on her clothes and grabbed a piece of gum from the back of her toiletries box. As she popped it into her mouth, she saw some motion out the bathroom window and frowned.

The hell was that?

A possum, she thought, leaning partly out the window to get a better look at the woods behind the trailer park. Dozens of them, coming out of the trees. Running.

Leaning further out, she saw the two…things…lurking at the edge of the woods, smiling with sharp teeth as the possums ran forward. She yelped, stumbling back.

"Whatsa matter?" Andy called, laughing. "You fall in?"

"Go piss outside, Andy!" she retorted, too startled by what she'd just seen to really think about the words.

No. She couldn't have seen that. Okay, she could've seen the possums—they might've been running from a coyote or something—but she *definitely* hadn't seen the people.

Or maybe someone was just playing a prank.

That was it. Probably one of Dylan's dumbass coworkers trying to get famous on YouTube.

She took a deep breath and peered outside again. The two human-possum-things were gone but the smaller animals remained. She heard Mr. Lyle, from the trailer off to the right, yowl in pain. Before she could call out, ask if he was all right, he stumbled out from his backyard—he kept a small potted garden—with one possum clinging to his leg, teeth sunk in deep, and two others attached to his arms. He tried in vain to hit them away with the trowel in his hand, but he was eighty-seven years old. He was strong from yard work, but not strong enough to fight off animals when he was already in pain.

He fell to his knees and then his face, one of the possums on his arms dislodging itself immediately to go for his neck.

Feeling sick, Alexis leaped to the door in her rush to open it, intent on warning Caleb and the others that they all needed to get the hell out of here. Then she heard a shout.

"The fuck is that, man?"

"I don't know!"

"Shut the goddamned door, Andy!"

"Fuckin' thing bit me!"

"Shoot it!"

The words were barely out before she heard a gunshot, then another, and then a third.

"How did you miss; it's ten feet away!"

"Andy, I told you to shut the door!"

Another gunshot, and then a scream of pain. Whether because whoever was holding the gun—probably Tanner; you'd think that handgun was his baby—had hit one of the others instead, or because someone else had been bitten, she didn't know.

And, she suddenly realized, she didn't want to find out.

The infatuated freshman, the senior in high school, or even the woman of two years ago would've rushed out of this room; would've risked everything to save her man.

That part of her was no longer more powerful than her own sense of self-preservation.

Grateful—for once—that Caleb had ignored something else she'd said and neglected to replace the torn-up screen in the bathroom window after it had finally fallen out, Alexis opened the window all the way, checking the ground for possums and the trees for those demon-looking people before she hauled herself outside, dropping to the ground with an 'oof'. The possums that were feeding on poor Mr. Lyle looked up at her and hissed, exposing bloody teeth.

It took everything she had to hold back a scream, but she knew if she called more attention to herself she'd never get out of here.

It had been over a decade since she'd been on the track team; almost seven years since she went for a run every morning.

Hopefully it was like riding a bike.

~~*

The car was silent for a few moments, as they waited for Vanessa to try and take in what he'd told her about Sophia and Tiffany.

Their first stop was to Henriette, Jeanne-Marie's granddaughter. For once, John was glad that most of the jobs available around here were minimum wage; it meant that Kendra was still living with her mother and they could hopefully rescue both of them at once.

"Now," Jeanne-Marie said softly, "would you be interested in hearing about this curse?"

"Right now, it'd make about as much sense as anything," John said grimly, swerving to hit a trio of possums that were chasing a dog. The dog charged away from the street into a nearby open backyard, and John hoped it'd make it. "First," he said, "do you or your Henriette have a landline? We might be able to call for help."

"And say what?" Vanessa asked, sounding on the verge of tears. "What are they going to do? Quarantine us? Bomb the whole town? I wouldn't put it past those assholes in charge and I know you don't either," she said. "That's if they even believe us in the first place."

"She's right," Jeanne-Marie said. "What needs to be done to fix this, the government and police can't do."

"All right," John said, wincing as another possum made a run across the road at exactly the wrong moment—right moment?—and bumped underneath the front right tire. "You said this has to do with your brother?"

"Yes. He's always been jealous, you see; I could believe it started while we were still in the womb. He was a golden child in my parents' eyes, but still he wanted more, and couldn't stand it when I got even the slightest affection or praise. He would make sure to punish me for it later."

Her expression darkened, and out of the corner of his eye John saw his niece reach forward from the backseat, resting a comforting hand on the old woman's arm. She was such a good kid, and Christian had tossed her aside. Hadn't called in seven years or tried to visit…hadn't even sent a birthday or Christmas card.

Yeah, he thought, he knew a thing or two about worthless brothers.

"Grandmother taught me some of her 'old family tricks'," Jeanne-Marie said. "Once Baptiste realized that, he started looking into hoodoo and such himself. But we hadn't seen each other in years; I thought it was finished. Then came mother's funeral last month, and he hadn't forgotten a thing. The anger was still…" She paused, took a deep, steadying breath. "Whatever he's done to me, it involves goofer dust."

Vanessa let out a high, nervous giggle. "It involves *what?*"

"Before you laugh again, miss, you should know it comes from the word 'kufwa'. That means 'to die'."

"Oh."

"I knew there was goofer dust because of how quick this came on," she said, motioning to her swollen legs. "It's common to mix it with dirt from your enemy's footprints, so it tends to affect the feet and legs first. And if that was the end of it, fine. I'd hobble my way to my brother's house if I had to and make him undo it. And I still will. But what he's done now…I don't know if it can be lifted so easily." Her eyes filled with tears as she looked around the deserted streets.

"What would've caused *this?*" John asked. "I don't…granted, I don't know much about witchcraft or hoodoo or whatever this is, but I've heard of curses and none of them involve attacking animals or…or turning people into animals."

"It was supposed to be a protection spell," Jeanne-Marie said, as they turned onto Henriette's street. "There was a possum, who came up onto my porch every night to snitch some food from the barn cats. Sweetest thing. And I…a couple of weeks ago, I found it in the road. Hit by a car. Had babies in its pouch, but none of them made it. And I just wanted to give them some protection, make it a little more likely that they knew to stay away from cars, knew to avoid traps. It was never supposed to do this. And it shouldn't have been able to. Even a mirror box shouldn't have this much strength," she murmured.

John pulled into Henriette's driveway, and Jeanne-Marie started to open the door.

"Don't; I'll go check," Vanessa said. "I can run if I need to."

"*We'll* check," John amended.

"All right," Jeanne-Marie said, though she pressed her nose to the window as the two of them got out and ran to the front door.

John pounded on the door, he and his niece sharing a worried look when there was no answer.

The car door opened behind them, and Vanessa turned. "Stay there!" she said, as John looked around, searching for any low-to-the-ground movements.

"The fourth rock on the left side of the sidewalk!" Jeanne-Marie called. "There's a key in it!"

Then she shut the door again, as Vanessa scurried to the fake rock and slid it open, pulling out the key. "Maybe the two of them just…just ran to the store or something?" she said hopefully, rejoining him at the door.

"I hope so," John said. "Stay behind me."

"Aunt Becca's the cop, not you," she muttered, though the humor in her voice fell flat as he unlocked the door and swung it open.

He relaxed at the sight of the sheet of computer paper taped to the floor in the entryway.

"GRANDMA- GONE TO CLINIC. WITH KENDRA AND MISS HOOPER.", it read.

He wondered for an instant why they hadn't just taped it to the door, but then he felt Vanessa's hand tense on his arm and looked back to see a possum next door, perched on the railing of Miss Hooper's porch.

He'd want to stay inside for as long as possible, too.

"Come on," Vanessa said, and the two of them ran for the car, shutting the doors before the possum could reach them.

"They went to the clinic," John said. "Along with their neighbor."

"Oh, good," Jeanne-Marie said. "Millie can't drive anymore; she'd need some looking after." She sighed. "I want to go back, make…make sure that they got there all right, but I need to get to Baptiste. If I can make him stop this—"

"I hope you can," John said. The idea of curses actually being real was unbelievable, but so was everything else that had happened today. "Gonna have to give me directions to his place, though."

Jeanne-Marie nodded. "I still know the way."

~~*

"This time, you stay in the car," Jeanne-Marie said, as John pulled into the dirt driveway. The road to Baptiste's house had several false stops and starts; he knew that

Rebecca had had to come out here repeatedly when people had filed complaints against him after he'd come into town and harassed them, and she'd complained about how it had somehow seemed to be at the end of a different country road every time.

Though Jeanne-Marie supported most of her weight on her cane, her stride was still determined as she walked up to her brother's door. "Baptiste!" she shouted, pounding on the door with her small fist. "Enough of this!"

John saw her shoulders tense in pain as she moved her cane away from her side and hit the door hard with it, trying to break through the flimsy wood. He opened the car door, but froze when she turned to him, a look of such command in her face that he nearly shrank back.

"Stay. In. The. Car," she ordered. Then she turned, hitting the door again with her cane, and again, until it broke enough that she was able to wrestle her hand inside and turn the lock.

She opened the door, began to step inside, and then let out a wail of pain.

Her warning forgotten, John ran to her side, Vanessa close behind him.

"Don't," he said, trying to push Vanessa back before she could see the body hanging from one of the tiny house's rafters, but it was too late. Vanessa gagged and stumbled back, and though he wanted to go to her, Jeanne-Marie collapsed against him, sobbing.

"Come on," he said, helping her away from the

doorway. Though she still looked like she was going to be sick, Vanessa moved back to Baptiste's door, pulling it shut so that Jeanne-Marie wouldn't still be within sight of her brother's body.

"We've got to call Aunt—" Vanessa began, and then she turned away, hugging herself tightly.

"Get back in the car," John told her softly. She'd feel better sitting down, and the area here was far too wooded for his liking.

Vanessa did so without complaining, and he knew that however the rest of their day went, this part was far from over. She'd be lucky if she didn't have nightmares for weeks.

And his niece wasn't the only one, he thought, as Jeanne-Marie struggled to get herself back under control.

"It's okay," he said. "I know he wasn't…didn't treat you well, but he was your brother. If you need to—"

"No. I can't. Not now," she said, straightening herself as best she could without the use of her cane, which she'd dropped just outside the door. He retrieved it for her, and as soon as he handed it back, she moved toward the house again.

"Jeanne-Marie…"

"Hush," she said, her voice still strained with tears. "I have to look for a mirror box, or hex bag, or…or whatever he used to do this."

"Let me—"

"You know what you're looking for, do you?"

"No," he admitted. He glanced back at the car, where Vanessa sat in the passenger seat with her head ducked down, shoulders shaking. He wanted to check on her, but neither did he want to leave Jeanne-Marie in that tiny house alone with her brother's corpse.

"Go see to your little girl," Jeanne-Marie said, and though tears still shone in her eyes her smile was gentle, and somehow calm, despite what lay beyond the door she now rested her hand on.

"You shouldn't have to do this."

"There are a lot of things I shouldn't have had to do, thanks to Baptiste. Blessedly, this should be the last."

She opened the door, leaving it open as she stepped inside. Despite the lingering smell, she rested her hand gently on her brother's leg.

It was a brief kindness—likely more than he deserved, and certainly more than anyone would be expected to give. Feeling like he'd intruded on a private moment, John went back to the car and got into the driver's seat.

"You okay?" he asked, because some questions were expected, even oddly comforting in their routine, even if you already knew the answer.

Vanessa shook her head, and John rubbed her back reassuringly.

"I guess we should've known," she muttered. "That *smell*. I mean, Baptiste came into the diner once in a while and he never did shower enough but…"

Maybe Jeanne-Marie had known, John thought. Even if she hadn't wanted to admit to herself. Maybe that was why she'd told him to stay in the car.

"I'm sorry," he said. Though he kept most of his focus on her, he also scanned the treeline, watching for anything moving toward the house or the car. "I wish you hadn't seen that."

"So do I," she said, trying to smile, though she sounded closer to crying than laughing. "Do you think this'll work? Whatever she's trying to do?"

"I hope so," he said. "Otherwise, I…"

He trailed off, but was sure she knew what he meant anyway. If this didn't work, then what did they try? Combing through the forest, searching for Sophia and Tiffany, praying that some gun-happy neighbor didn't panic and shoot them first?

John closed his eyes briefly, trying to push thoughts of Sophia away, as traitorous as that felt. If he thought too much about what had happened to her, *what* she was…

Then Jeanne-Marie hobbled out of the house, looking so old and exhausted that he half-expected the light breeze to blow her away.

"It's not there," she murmured, by way of greeting as she climbed into the backseat. "Nothing I need is there."

"Then where would it be?" John asked.

"I don't know."

"Think, please," Vanessa whispered. "Or Tiffany…Sophia…"

"Drive," Jeanne-Marie said, clutching the top of her cane hard in both hands. "It always helped me concentrate. And I—I have to be away from here."

John nodded, driving away from Baptiste's grim home and back into town.

He was heading toward the clinic when a young woman darted out in front of his car, reminding him of nothing so much as a deer fleeing into the road with no regard for what dangers might be waiting.

John swerved, slamming on the brakes, and ended up clipping her in the leg instead of striking her head-on. She hit the ground and rolled, shrieking in pain, and Vanessa was out of the car almost before he'd fully stopped. He followed her out.

"Shit," Vanessa whispered. "Come on, Alexis."

The two of them tried to help her to her feet. She crumpled as soon as she started to put weight on her right leg.

"Uncle John," Vanessa said, staring in horror behind Alexis. A group of at least fifty possums were racing toward them. No wonder she hadn't been looking where she was going.

Knowing Alexis wouldn't be able to get to the car fast enough on her own two feet, John picked her up, wincing when she yelped at the contact to her right leg.

"Sorry," he said, hurrying her to the car as Vanessa opened the back passenger door for her. Alexis climbed in, dragging her wounded leg, and John shut the door behind her, turning around just as one of the faster possums went for his foot. He kicked it, feeling its teeth scrape against its shoe. Vanessa shouted for him, and he got into the car, making a U-turn across three lawns to turn back and run over a good number of the possum group that had been pursuing Alexis.

"You okay?" Vanessa asked, holding Alexis's hand tightly as the other woman closed her eyes and keened, whether in pain from her leg or the feeling of bumping over so many bodies, John didn't know.

"Yeah. Yeah," Alexis said.

"And Caleb?" John asked. Rebecca had had to keep Caleb and his friends overnight for drunk and disorderly a few times, and Alexis had always been there to bail Caleb out. The two of them had been joined at the hip since high school; Ness had told him that every Monday and Wednesday until Caleb had lost his job, they'd come to the Sunny Side Up Diner for breakfast.

Alexis's expression seemed to close down. "Didn't make it. None of the guys did."

"I'm sorry," Vanessa whispered.

"Don't be. I'm the one who left them there," she said, and then her shuttered expression disappeared in a flurry of tears.

~~*

When they got back to the clinic, it was to find at

least a dozen more cars in the parking lot than had been there when they'd left. Several of them weren't anywhere close to actual parking spots, and John wondered how panicked the drivers had been, how desperate to get inside.

If anything else had gotten inside, too.

Alexis was still crying. Vanessa was hugging her, talking soothingly, though she sounded near tears herself. Beside him, Jeanne-Marie was staring out the window, lost in thought. When he opened his door, she startled, only then seeming to realize they were at the clinic.

While he moved around to the back passenger side to help Alexis, Jeanne-Marie got out and made her way to her truck.

"Where are you going?" he called.

"Home!" she said. "I can't find the hex bag, so I'm going to cast a counter-curse, and take a cleansing bath. That ought to break any curse he laid on me. I hope," she finished quietly.

"I'll go with you," Vanessa said.

"Ness."

"You need to be here for Aunt Becca," she told him. "And…and for Tiffany and Sophia, if somebody finds them. I can't go sit in the clinic and wait," she confessed. "I can't."

He hesitated, but finally nodded, as Alexis looped her arm over his shoulders and gingerly got to her feet, resting most of her weight on her good leg. "Be careful." He looked across the cars again and paused. He recognized that vehicle. "Wait a minute," he called. "The Stewarts are here. They'll have better weapons than just a cane."

Vanessa nodded, and she and Jeanne-Marie got into the truck, shutting the doors as they waited. He helped Alexis into the clinic.

The front waiting room seemed to contain half the town, though he knew it was only about thirty people—the Stewarts were just that animated.

"Joyce!" he called, seeing the nurse off to the left, giving a teenager an ice pack for a black eye. She said a few words to the young man, then hurried to them, frowning at the sight of Alexis's leg.

"What happened?" she asked.

"I hit her with my car," John said. "Though, to be fair, she did run right out in front of me." He glanced down at her, and to his relief, she tried to return his encouraging smile.

"Our beds are full up," Joyce said, as he looked around the room again, searching. "Your wife's doing fine. Olivia is realigning her arm," she said, before returning her attention to Alexis. "Did you get bitten? Scratched?"

"No," Alexis said.

"Have you seen changes in people who were?" John asked. "Been able to do anything for them?"

"Been able to lock them up in the back storeroom is what we've been able to do," Joyce said. "Never seen anything like it before in my life. Come on, sweetie," she told Alexis. "I wish I could give you better than some sheets on the floor, but that's what we've got right now. Neela!" she called, and a nurse who was finishing stitching up a cut above a patient's eye paused and looked up. "When you're done, I need help over here!"

The patient Neela was stitching was Benjamin Stewart. The front end of their truck had been pretty crunched in when he'd seen it in the parking lot; the cut had probably been sustained then. Danny was sitting next to him, along with Jake, the eldest son.

"Danny," he called, making his way through the crowd to the other man's side once Neela and Joyce had Alexis. "I need weapons."

Danny glanced up, a faint grin on his face. "That's such a nice sentence to hear."

"Over here," Benjamin said, getting to his feet, and walking a few steps to where a giant duffel bag was crammed under a chair.

"You okay?" John asked, when he stumbled a little as he leaned down.

"Oh yeah, this is nothing," Benjamin said. "You should've seen the stitches I had to get when I fell off the tire swing. Hit a chunk of brick that was half-hidden in the dirt. Remember that, dad?"

"I do, I do," Danny said.

Then Benjamin unzipped the bag, and for a few seconds it was all John could do to stare at the contents. He'd been expecting it to be full of guns, but instead he saw duct tape, knives, empty beer bottles, boxes of nails, cans of hairspray, and—

"What are those?"

"Potato guns!" Danny said proudly. "And now I'm sorry for your childhood."

"Any actual guns?"

Danny snorted. "My kids've been doing stupid shit since they could crawl. Like hell am I keeping guns in the house."

Fair, John thought, picking up one of the cans of hairspray with a questioning look.

"Good choice," Benjamin said. "Grab that, and a lighter, and you've got yourself a homemade flamethrower."

John smiled, taking the lighter that Danny handed him.

"Here," Kathleen-Rose said, and John jumped at her sudden presence at his side. He remembered her as a little girl, clambering around everywhere along with her brothers and shrieking like a banshee. Now, for all that she and most of her siblings had taken after her father's heavy body type, both she and Kyle could move like ghosts. He looked up at her, and saw that she was holding a mop handle that had a butcher knife duct-taped to the end.

"I've made a bunch of them," she said, pointing to the corner of the room. Several of these makeshift weapons were leaning against the wall, along with a couple of boards with nails driven through and the now-classic bats with barbed wire wrapped around them.

"Thanks," he said, taking the weapon.

She nodded, giving him a shy smile before she headed back to the corner, putting on a pair of leather gloves before she got to work on another bat.

He went back outside, checking around as he went to Jeanne-Marie's truck, ducking down to look under vehicles before he left the front sidewalk. Seeing nothing, at least for now, he went around to the passenger side and gave Vanessa the weapons.

"Got a proper bodyguard now," Jeanne-Marie said. She met his eyes and gave a brief nod, a silent 'I'll watch out for her, too'.

He watched them drive away, unable to shake the feeling that he was making a terrible mistake.

Both Sophia and Vanessa were out of their sight. They were supposed to protect them, and now all they could do was pray.

He turned to go back inside, seeing that Danny and Kathleen-Rose were both handing out weapons to anybody still in good enough shape to hold one.

"Where are Kyle and Tim?" he asked, wondering if Danny was in the same boat he was in.

Hell, Melanie might not even know that her family was in this much danger. She was gone for a week-long business conference, and since the phone lines were down…

"Oh, they're fine," Danny said breezily. "Why we came here in the first place. Timmy stayed overnight, so we came to keep an eye on him what with all this going on."

"Is he okay?"

"He will be, he's just miserable at both ends right now, if you catch my drift. He ate some raw pork on a dare—least he got a hundred bucks out of it, though I told him he was gonna be using it to pay off part of the doctor bill. Kyle's keeping watch outside the door. Lock's busted and nobody needs to walk in on that."

"Kinda sorry I asked," John said, and Danny laughed, clapping him on the shoulder. "How 'bout your girls?"

"Vanessa's with Miss Jeanne-Marie," John said. "She thinks she…well, that she may be able to stop this somehow."

"Witchcraft," Danny said, nodding sagely. "Or hoodoo, rather, I think she calls it."

"You knew about all this?"

"Oh yeah!" Danny said. "I've been asking her to cast protection spells for the kids ever since Jake tried to cram a battery up his nose when he was a toddler."

"She thinks her brother did something to her spells," John said, unable to believe that was actually a sentence coming out of his mouth. "Reversed them?"

Danny's face grew solemn. "You think my kids might be in trouble?"

"Yeah. But not much more than all of us, for whatever that's worth," John said, as he heard somebody closer to the front of the room shriek. Looking toward the sound, he saw a large possum banging itself against the front lobby door, leaving a smear of blood and saliva as its teeth clashed against the glass.

There wasn't much chance of that single possum breaking through, but when several others joined it within the next couple of minutes, all of them throwing their bodies against the door, people began to chatter nervously. Some of the smaller kids started crying.

Danny climbed up onto one of the empty chairs—most people weren't sitting anymore, but were rather pacing as best they could or watching the door nervously—and raised his voice. "Hey!" he shouted, until at least most of the crowd turned to him. "They get through there, I don't care what kind of weapons we've made, somebody's gonna get bit. This place has got a tornado shelter, right?"

"Right, but it's outside," Joyce said. "Just got put in about five years ago; we don't have a basement."

"Then we'll make a run for it before we lose our chance," Danny said.

"Some of us, anyway," Alexis said.

"Not gonna leave you here alone," Danny said. "We'll get everybody who can't move quick into one or two of the patient rooms, ones without windows if we can. And my kids and I'll stay in here with you, make sure you stay safe," he said, glancing around at his gathered children.

John smiled. Danny's enthusiasm made a lot of

people dismiss him as childish, but he and Melanie ran a large, boisterous household—he knew how to take charge when need be.

Trying his best to ignore the angry hisses from outside, he went down the hall of patient rooms. All of the doors were open, the better to keep an eye on everything, and he nearly bumped into Olivia as she hurried out of his wife's room to check on another patient.

As he came in, Becca got to her feet, her arm now in a splint. She walked straight to him, burying her face in the crook of his neck and hugging him as best she could.

"Sophia?" she whispered.

"Not yet," he said. "We'll find her, Becca. Or Jeanne-Marie will get this taken care of." He paused, wondering how to explain all that to his wife. For all that he considered himself no-nonsense, liable to scoff at ghost-hunter shows or the very idea of magic, Rebecca was even more so. "There's some weird shit going on—" he finally began, only to have her look up at him with a deadpan expression.

"Really? I hadn't noticed."

He smiled and kissed her, feeling her lips curve into a smile as she kissed him back. Then she moved away, heading to the side table where the nurse had put her holster and sidearm. Not bothering with the holster, she picked up the gun with her good hand.

Her left wasn't the dominant one, he thought, and she'd complained before about not being as good a shot with it. But better than not being able to shoot at all.

"Anyone who can run is going to hide in the tornado shelter," he said.

She nodded, walking with him out to the main room. The possums had gotten through the first glass door and were now in the small lobby, crashing against the last pane of glass separating them from the waiting room and their would-be prey with renewed frenzy.

"The hell is that?" someone yelled, pointing outside. John saw a furry creature run by on two legs, though the distance was great enough that he was unsure if it was his daughter, Tiffany, or some other poor person who'd been bitten.

"You didn't know?" someone else exclaimed. "My sister-in-law got bit, and started turning into one of the damn things on the car ride over! I kicked her out before she could finish changing. I love her and all, but I got limits."

"My daughter was bitten," Becca announced loudly, and most eyes turned to her. "I know all of you are scared. But we can't panic. I absolutely encourage killing all the little ones we can. But there may be some way to help the ones who've been turned. As long as there's a chance we can get our friends, our neighbors, back, then we're going to take it. Evade if possible, capture if possible. And if any one of you hurts my daughter, I will shoot you in the face."

"Hey now," Eric Liston protested, his voice a reasonable facsimile of lighthearted. "I pay your salary."

The joke wasn't very good, but his terrified gaze was locked on the door, so they let it pass, and most even chuckled.

"All right," Danny said. "These things are fuckin' smart. If we all gather at the back door, they're gonna follow. We stay here as long as we can, let these little bastards think they're still about to get a free meal, and then on my signal we run like hell for the back door and to the shelter. Okay?"

"I'll pass word to the patients," Joyce said. "And then I'll get the remaining ones into one room, if possible. I'm staying with them."

Neela hurried after her as she started toward the patient hall, keeping her voice low.

"Are you sure?" she murmured. "I know about your whole animal thing."

Joyce's gaze automatically went to her arm. Covered by her scrubs was a messy scar on her shoulder, from where she'd tried to comfort the family dog during a thunderstorm. She'd toddled up to it and hugged its head tightly, and it had lashed out and bitten her. She didn't have a phobia of dogs, per se, but her heart rate had always gotten uncomfortably fast around any animal that had the potential to turn on her. Seeing those creatures just outside, teeth snapping…

At the start, yes, it had been all she could do to keep from hyperventilating. But the group outside would be out of danger once they got across that short stretch of lawn.

Her most vulnerable patients would have much flimsier doors between themselves and this threat. They needed her.

"My mom was an ICU nurse for 30 years up in Kansas City," she said. "before she retired and moved us down here. Strongest woman you'd ever hope to meet. I'm gonna live up to her example today."

CHAPTER NINE

She'd never seen anything like the inside of Jeanne-Marie's house.

The older woman went to start running a bath, and Vanessa wandered around the living room with an awed smile on her face, her fear momentarily forgotten. One whole wall was taken up with built-in bookshelves, and while most did hold books, several shelves were set aside for jars and bottles, and a few intricately-painted animal skulls.

"Did you do these?" she asked, gingerly tracing an intricate line of black paint with her fingertip. "They're beautiful."

"Been years ago now, but yes," Jeanne-Marie said, as she headed into the kitchen and opened up a can of cat food. Three cats immediately streaked past Vanessa, meowing. "Don't think my arthritis would enjoy it if I picked up a brush that small now. I mixed up everything in these jars, too," she said proudly, moving to Vanessa's side.

"What's this?" Vanessa asked, focusing on one jar in particular. It was enormous; nearly scraped the top of the shelf, and it was full to the brim. In the liquid, she could see rose petals, a vanilla bean, and a couple of cinnamon sticks. There were other leaves, but she wasn't quite sure what they were.

"Fast Luck oil," Jeanne-Marie said, as she selected various jars and bottles, the Fast Luck Oil among them, and set them down on her coffee table. "Take those to the bathroom?"

Vanessa did so, then followed Jeanne-Marie as she hobbled into the kitchen and took a pot out of a lower cabinet. One of the cats hissed at her and took off for less stranger-infested parts of the house; another came over to sniff curiously at her pants leg; and the third took the opportunity to steal what little remained of the others' food.

"Be a dear and fetch me that storm water," Jeanne-Marie said, pointing to a jar of water that was on a high shelf. "Don't feel up to hopping on my stool right now."

"Got it," Vanessa said, taking one more look out the window to make sure there was nothing out the ordinary before she got the jar down.

Jeanne-Marie poured all of the contents into the pot. "All right," she said, motioning to the spice cabinet. "Now for the 13 herbs. Agrimony, please?"

Vanessa stared at the vast collection of dried spices and leaves, very few of which seemed to be labeled. "Um."

"Kids," Jeanne-Marie muttered, though there wasn't any heat to it. She moved past her and grabbed two bottles, searching through for more. "Put these next to the stove," she said, handing her bottle after bottle. A few of them had been marked with a type-in label maker—juniper, rosemary, bay leaves—but most were either blank or had clearly had a label pulled off, judging by the strip of residue.

"Kendra doesn't know how to identify her herbs either. She bought a whole mess of conditioning oils online, if you can believe it. Now granted, some look like they were made by people who knew what they were doing, but others, I swear they just ran tap water into a bottle and added wintergreen oil for smell. She said she wasn't going to use any of them, it was more for the 'aesthetic'."

Vanessa ferried thirteen bottles as she spoke, setting them next to where the pot was heating before she returned to watching the windows. She'd set down the hairspray and the lighter on the table by the front door, but had picked up the makeshift spear again.

"So what exactly are you doing?" she asked.

"Rue, agrimony, and several of these others are cursebreakers," Jeanne-Marie said, plucking out leaves, stems, and in one case what looked like a little chunk of bark, and dropping them into the pot. "13 herbs, boiled for 13 minutes. Then I'll use the oils. Hey!" she said, when one of her cats leaped up onto the counter. She picked up a large spray bottle and held it out, nozzle pointing toward the cat. She didn't have to even spritz it with the water; it flattened its ears for a second and then hopped back down.

"Will all this work?" Vanessa asked.

"Only guarantee in spellwork is that there aren't guarantees," Jeanne-Marie told her. "Now go shut off the bath, please, and then hush. I have to pray for this part."

Vanessa nodded, shutting off the bathwater and then listening to Jeanne-Marie's muttered prayers as she continued her vigil.

She didn't see anything until Jeanne-Marie was straining the mixture into a different pot. As she carried the liquid into the bathroom, Vanessa called her name.

"They're coming."

"Well, that's what you've got weapons for, I imagine," Jeanne-Marie said, though her voice wasn't nearly as carefree as her words. "How close?"

"About fifty feet," Vanessa said. "Four or—no, five of them. I think they're more interested in the chickens than in the house."

Jeanne-Marie turned. "I never brought them inside. How...how close did you say?"

Vanessa started to answer, but then realized that the look on her face was genuine distress. Granted, she herself had never thought of chickens as potential pets, but of course Jeanne-Marie would be close to these. "You go take your bath, I'll bring them in."

"You ever picked up a chicken?"

"No, but it's better than just standing here and watching them get attacked."

"Not if...if you get attacked, too. I won't allow it. You stay in the house."

"But—"

"I mean it, now."

With that, she went into the bathroom and closed

the door behind her. Vanessa watched the possums charge the chicken coop, listened to the chickens' panicked squawks as they flapped their wings in warning, and then she turned away.

First they had to chew through the coop wire. That might buy them some time.

Her gaze moved to the hairspray and lighter.

Screw it, she thought, trading out the mop-knife spear for the other weapon. Jeanne-Marie had already confronted the body of her brother today; she didn't need to listen to her pets die.

Double-checking that there were still only five, and that their full attention was on the chicken coop, Vanessa slipped outside, readying her weapon.

She couldn't take them entirely by surprise, she realized. If she aimed this thing at them right now, she'd risk hurting the chickens, too.

Speaking of risk, she'd never done anything like this. What if she tried to light this thing and the flame just came back to the hairspray bottle somehow and exploded?

Maybe she should've brought the spear instead.

Too late now, she thought, as one of them turned and hissed at her. The others followed suit, and Vanessa aimed the hairspray, holding the lighter in front of and just below it, hoping that Jeanne-Marie's prayers might cover her, too.

She burned three in her first spray, and the two who were untouched ran away, whatever odd force making them act like this apparently not stronger than the primal fear of fire.

Two of the ones she hit were dead. The third stumbled around in a half-circle, then dropped to the ground, twitching in pain for a few seconds before going still.

"Shit," Vanessa muttered. She knew it was necessary, but…

She looked up then, and saw the two who had run away were coming back with reinforcements.

A lot of them.

"Shit!" she said again—she could almost feel Aunt Becca swatting her on the back of the head—and looked to the chickens. She couldn't bring them in, not fast enough.

Might as well give them a fighting chance, she thought, shoving the lighter into her pocket and then opening the coop door. She charged up the steps and into the house, slamming and locking the door behind her.

Locking it. Because of course they could open doors, she thought.

"Jeanne-Marie!" she called. "Might want to hurry up!"

"Was that the front door I heard?"

"…no?"

"Don't be lying, I'm a lot more practiced at it than you are. What's outside?"

"The good news is, your chickens seem okay. Bad news, there's a *lot* more possums now and they really want in."

Silence for a moment, as the possums outside clambered on top of each other to try and reach the windows.

"Come in here," Jeanne-Marie said.

"Are you sure?" Vanessa said. "If they—"

"Now, please."

She hurried into the bathroom to find the bathwater draining. Jeanne-Marie was sitting on a small chair next to the tub, wearing a loose white dress, several of the jars she'd brought in earlier still open at her side. She wasn't sure how to describe the smell in the room—all of the herbs and oils seemed to crash together in the tiny, steam-filled space.

"I would like to use some of these on you, too, if you're amenable."

"I…" Vanessa said. "Don't I have to believe, or something?"

Jeanne-Marie smiled. "I'll do the believing."

"Sure, okay," Vanessa finally said. She was a dyed-in-the-wool "spiritual but not religious!" cliche; if this would help the older woman to feel better, she couldn't see the harm in it.

And honestly, at this point she was pretty sure it'd help her feel better, too. She might not believe herself, but she could see the reverence Jeanne-Marie had for her materials and her rituals, and it was oddly reassuring.

"What do I do?" she asked, peering at the open jars.

"You hold still," Jeanne-Marie said. She dipped her fingertip into the one Vanessa had asked about earlier—Fast Luck—and then pressed a dot of it onto each of her palms.

"Rub that in," she said. "I'm going to use a couple more— Blessing, and Protection—and then I want you to see if those little beasts are gone."

Vanessa nodded, waiting as Jeanne-Marie dotted the two oils onto her forehead.

"What…what others did you use?" she asked, suddenly afraid that when she opened the door, she'd be met with a furry wall of teeth.

"Most of them were to end a curse, or to send it right back where it came from," Jeanne-Marie said. "Jinx Killer, Cast Off Evil, Reversing; Uncrossing…I also used Cut and Clear," she said, holding up a small jar that smelled of lemons, "to break any lingering relationship with my twin, including, I hope, his ability to make a curse stay with me."

"Shouldn't he have lost any ability when—well, I mean…"

"Dying words and wishes can be incredibly powerful," Jeanne-Marie told her, her expression gentling. "Open the door, Vanessa."

She grimaced and picked up the spear, flinging the door open with a yell.

There was nothing there.

Feeling more than a little silly now, she moved out

of the bathroom, feeling a bud of hope bloom when she saw no possums trying to scratch at the windows.

She started to tell Jeanne-Marie that they were gone, but then spun in a full circle and looked at the ceiling, because if it was one thing Uncle John's horror movies had taught her, it was that the minute she said everything was okay, she'd get ambushed.

There was nothing.

"It might have worked," she said.

She moved to the window, and saw the enormous group of possums running away. The sight would've been reassuring, if Tiffany and Sophia hadn't been at the front of the group, leading them at a dead run back towards town.

Vanessa didn't know how she knew, but she was absolutely certain that they were heading toward the clinic.

"Jeanne-Marie…"

"I know," she said. "Hold on. I'm going to get a few things for the road." She put lids back on a couple of the jars—Blessing and Protection—and brought them out, then shut the bathroom door to make sure the cats didn't get into any of the open ones.

Vanessa peered outside, not seeing any possums remaining on the porch. "Truck keys?" she asked. "I'll get it running and then help you get stuff out there."

Jeanne-Marie nodded to a key holder on the wall. "Far left."

Vanessa took the keys and opened the door, screaming when a possum that had been pressed against the door charged at her. She stumbled back and jabbed at it with the knife at the end of the mop handle, grazing its shoulder before it dodged and came for her legs again. She yelped and jumped up onto one of Jeanne-Marie's chairs, stabbing down at it as Jeanne-Marie went for the bathroom. Instead of shutting herself inside, as she'd expected, she came right back out, clutching a jar to her chest.

Vanessa risked a glance at the open door, afraid that more would come in and head for Jeanne-Marie, but fortunately there were no more to be found. She stabbed down at the possum again, but the knife just embedded itself in the floor when the possum turned toward the kitchen when something clattered in there.

"Look out!" Vanessa yelled, as the possum charged toward the other room. Before it could get there, Jeanne-Marie stepped out of the kitchen, holding the spray bottle from the kitchen counter. She sprayed it at the rushing animal, hitting it in the face. The possum hissed and yowled, stopping in its tracks and pawing at its eyes.

Vanessa finally succeeded in yanking the knife out of the hardwood floor and stabbed the possum in the back of the neck, killing it as quickly as she could. She'd wanted to just run out of the house and leave it there, but if it recovered and got to the cats…

"What did you put in there?" Vanessa asked, as she raced ahead of her to the truck, carrying the keys and the hairspray in one hand, and the spear in her other.

"Fiery Wall of Protection oil!" Jeanne-Marie

hooted. "Homemade pepper spray. Might not be the traditional way to use it, but it worked!"

"It did," Vanessa laughed. She put the hairspray in the truck and started the engine, then checked the backseat and the flatbed (because if she died for ignoring the "the killer's in the backseat!" trope, Uncle John would contact her via Ouija board just to tease her about it for the rest of her afterlife).

Jeanne-Marie unloaded the jars she was carrying into the middle front seat. "Come on across here now," she said, when Vanessa started to get in on the passenger side. "You drive."

Vanessa didn't bother asking for an explanation. Whether she had spellwork to do or just wanted to rest for a few minutes before they got back into the fight, it didn't matter. They had to get to the clinic.

As she drove, Jeanne-Marie opened one of the smaller jars, talking softly as she pressed one droplet to her forehead, and one to each of her eyelids.

Then she fell silent, and Vanessa drove as fast as she felt she safely could, which wasn't much over the usual speed limit—she couldn't help but recall Alexis running right in front of the car.

When she glanced back over at Jeanne-Marie, her eyes were open again, and tears were running down her face.

"Jeanne-Marie?" she asked, pulling the truck over. "Hey. Hey," she said, raising her voice and grabbing one of her hands when she didn't answer. "What's wrong?"

"We need to go to the graveyard," she whispered, her voice hoarse. "I know where the hex bag is."

CHAPTER ELEVEN

"Vanessa?" Jeanne-Marie asked, once her expression wasn't so dazed. "I said the graveyard."

"I know," Vanessa said. "But I'm assuming if the hex bag is there, that it's buried someplace?"

"Yes."

"We can get shovels from the caretaker's shed, but we're gonna need help, being out in the open like that. At least three other people to dig, while I keep watch. You should stay in the truck. If anything happens to you, none of the rest of us know what to do with...with any of this stuff," she said, motioning to the jars.

"You're right," Jeanne-Marie said. "We'll...oh, God."

Vanessa had been focusing on parking as close to the clinic doors as she could without bumping into someone else's poorly-parked car. Now she followed Jeanne-Marie's gaze, and saw the glass lobby doors had been shattered. Possums wandered the now-empty waiting room, nipping at each other in lieu of not having any human victims.

Vanessa threw open the door, stepping out onto the parking lot. "Uncle John! Aunt Becca!"

"Get back in here," Jeanne-Marie hissed, as a dozen pairs of beady eyes turned toward her. Reluctantly, she obeyed, slamming the door behind her and then ducking her head down to take several deep breaths.

"None of them would've just sat there while those things broke in," Jeanne-Marie said. "I'm sure they're all right. Probably holed up in one of the patient rooms."

"So what do we do?"

"It'll take longer than I'd like, but we'll just have to dig."

Vanessa nodded and reached for the keys, but then one of the possums was rocketed across the lobby by the force of a...

"Potato?" she whispered, as another round missile struck, and then another, and another.

She rolled down the window, grinning when she heard Danny Stewart's unmistakable holler of pride.

"How d'ya like *that*, you little bastards?"

Another potato struck a possum that charged toward their voices, and Vanessa heard Kathleen-Rose as she got back out of the truck.

"I got one!" the girl exclaimed.

"Good job, sweetie!"

"Mr. Stewart!" Vanessa called. "We need help!"

"Be right there!" he yelled, and after a few minutes—and several more fired potatoes—he and Kathleen-Rose and Benjamin came into sight, stepping gingerly into the glass-and-dead-possum littered lobby.

"Where's everybody else?" Vanessa asked. "Are they all right?"

"They're fine, it's okay," Danny said, clapping her

on the shoulder. "Ben! That one's not dead!"

"Got it," Benjamin said, hefting his barbed-wire-wrapped bat. Vanessa looked away, focusing on Danny and Kathleen-Rose instead.

"Most of the town's down in the tornado shelter behind the building there," he said. "About ten people in one of the patient rooms."

She heard a high-pitched, inhuman cry from behind her, and her heart sank as she turned to see Tiffany and Sophia, leading a flood of possums down the street toward them. Several other changed humans were among the crowd, and Vanessa blinked back tears.

What if they couldn't bring them back?

"Oh shit," Danny whispered. "Kids! Get everything we've got!"

"No, no!" Vanessa exclaimed. "We've got to get to the graveyard! Jeanne-Marie knows how to stop this!"

"That many of them? They'll break through the patient room door in five minutes," Danny said. "We're staying."

"…no we're not," Benjamin said. "Come on! Get the sheets from the floor!" He charged back across the lobby. Vanessa scooped up several sheets, shaking bits of broken glass off them. She glanced back, seeing that Jeanne-Marie was rolling the window back up on the truck and then ducking out of sight. Good.

She ran after the Stewarts as Benjamin pounded on the door to the tune of Shave and a Haircut. Kyle opened the door, his eyes widening when he saw the look on his brother's face.

"Too many of 'em coming. We're moving everybody out," Benjamin said.

"If you can, carry someone in your arms," Danny said, picking up his youngest son in one arm and hefting a duffel bag in the other.

Vanessa focused hard on Tim for a few seconds—pale and scared—her eyes filling with tears. He was in Sophia's class. Her age. Sophia should be in this room with him, helping to comfort everyone, rattling off bizarre animal knowledge to keep them distracted.

"Ness!"

"Huh?" she asked, looking to Danny.

"Use the sheets as stretchers. Drag someone to the shelter if you have to. Come on!"

Danny ran then, heading out the back door with Tim. Benjamin picked up Alexis, who didn't grimace at the motion—they must've been able to give her some good painkillers while they'd been gone—and Kathleen-Rose took Penny McKenzie's six-year-old (who was in for a fractured foot). Penny followed them to the back door, walking as fast as her nine months of pregnancy would allow.

Vanessa laid out a sheet, helping Neela to lift old Mr. Ross, using the sheets from his bed to cradle him as they set him down the sheets on the floor. His daughter came into the diner sometimes; he'd had hip surgery in

Kansas City and come back here for some physical therapy. He was able to walk for a few minutes with the aid of a walker now, but running to the shelter was out of the question.

"One, two, three!" Neela said, and she and Vanessa each lifted an end, carrying Mr. Ross out the back door, doing their best not to bump him on either side (Neela had more upper arm strength, and Vanessa wasn't used to carrying anyone like this: the blanket swayed more than any of them would like).

By the time they got to the shelter, the door was open, the people inside ushering in those who'd needed extra help. Uncle John was helping Penny McKenzie down the steps, and he grinned when he looked up and saw her.

"Vanessa!"

She grinned back, would have waved if her hands weren't occupied.

They got Mr. Ross to the shelter, where many hands were waiting to help get him down safely. Once he was taken care of, Neela went down to be with the patients, while Joyce and her aunt and uncle came up. Danny traded weapons with some of the people inside the shelter, getting longer-range things while trading some of the shorter-range ones that were still in the duffel bag.

"You stay in the shelter," he told his oldest, Jake. "Keep an eye on them. We'll be back as soon as we can."

Jake nodded, retreating underground.

"Watch your arm," Vanessa said, when Becca

passed her gun to Danny and hugged her tight to her good side. "We have to get to the graveyard. Jeanne-Marie'll take us there."

They ran around to the front of the building, only to see that the possums had reached the parking lot. Several were surrounding Jeanne-Marie's truck, doing their best to chew on the tires.

"Dad!" Kathleen-Rose exclaimed. "No fair; you said I could use one!"

"I'm sure you'll get a chance," he said, and Vanessa turned, her mouth dropping open when she saw him lighting a hunk of fabric that was stuck down inside a half-full liquor bottle.

"Is that a Molotov cocktail?" she squeaked, and Danny cast her a quick grin before he threw it into the biggest concentration of possums.

Then Benjamin yelped as a hand shot out from under Jeanne-Marie's car, claws sinking into his ankle and yanking forward, pulling him onto his back.

"Ben!" Danny exclaimed.

Sophia crawled out from under the truck, snarling at all of them. With a wordless cry, her aunt nearly dropped her gun, and Vanessa pulled her back.

"Sophia," John said quietly. "Sophia, honey. Hey, it's us. You have to recognize us. Please."

She growled, crouching down in preparation for a spring. Benjamin lashed out with one arm, knocking her into the side of the truck. She whimpered and shook her head, then sprang for him before he could fully get to his feet, sinking her teeth into his shoulder.

Kathleen-Rose let out a panicked cry and raised her own weapon, a broom handle with a broken beer bottle duct-taped to it. She jabbed it at Sophia's face, and the other girl retreated with a hiss, just enough to let Benjamin scoot back. Danny started to help him up, but Benjamin shrugged him off.

"Get in the truck!" he snapped. "You know what's gonna happen to me!"

Kathleen-Rose kept aiming the broken glass at Sophia, keeping her away while the rest of her family climbed into the bed of the pickup. Vanessa joined them back there, while Rebecca climbed into the middle seat and John got in next to her, starting the truck.

"Come on!" Danny said, holding out his hands for his daughter. Kathleen-Rose glanced to her older brother, who had his eyes shut tightly, breathing hard, as white fur began to poke out of his skin. Giving one last jab at Sophia, she tossed her weapon to Vanessa and grabbed her father's hands.

As he pulled her into the truck bed, Sophia grabbed hold of her ankle.

"Dad!" she shrieked.

Joyce grabbed hold of Kathleen-Rose as well, hauling her forward. Kathleen-Rose lashed out desperately with her other foot, kicking Sophia in the nose. The three of them stumbled into the rest of the small group as the blow forced Sophia to let go.

"Did she scratch me?" Kathleen-Rose asked, her voice high with hysteria. "Did she?"

"Here, sit, sit," Danny said. "Breathe. Let me check." He tugged down her sock, searching the area where Sophia had grabbed. "I don't think so. It's a little red but the skin isn't broken. Here, it's okay," he said, hugging her as she collapsed forward, crying. "I know what'll help."

He motioned for the duffel bag, which Vanessa slid over. He took out a half-full bottle of whiskey and a lighter. Kathleen-Rose rubbed at her eyes, grinning.

"Part of the pack's following the truck," he said. "Light 'em up."

Just before she did so, Vanessa saw Sophia join the group that Tiffany led out of the hospital. Dozens and dozens of people who had been changed, their faces and bodies distorted by whatever awful spell Baptiste had managed to cast, or corrupt.

"Dammit," Joyce whispered. "They found the group we had in quarantine."

Then they all held on as John accelerated, turning toward the cemetery.

They stopped at the caretaker's shed, grabbing all the shovels they could, both for digging and weapon purposes. At Jeanne-Marie's instruction, after they were all back in the truck John pulled to a stop next to a pair of graves with two small, simple headstones. Jeanne-Marie got out and hobbled to the one on the left. "This one," she said quietly. "The hex bag is in here."

Vanessa moved to her side, staring at the names in horror. "These are your parents?"

"Yes."

"How did…"

"At the funeral," Jeanne-Marie said. "Baptiste made a big fuss about how our father was already gone, and how he'd apologized over and over to me for his 'misspent youth' but nothing seemed to matter. How he'd wished that I'd softened my heart toward him, that we'd been able to put everything behind us, while our mother was still alive. All this, when the only times he ever bothered to visit were when he thought she might have money for him. But every time he came by…mom thought he hung the moon."

"What an ass," Vanessa said, and this time she actually did feel the light swat on the back of her head. She glanced back at her aunt, who raised an eyebrow at her.

"He put a box in the coffin, in her arms. Mementos, he said, of the two of us. Said we'd be together there, at least, and maybe give our parents' spirits some rest. I thought he was just getting in one last insult, giving our aunt and uncles another reason to hate me. I should have checked in the box," she said, as Danny, Kathleen-Rose, and John began to dig. "He had everything prepared. Then his death set it in motion."

Vanessa gave the older woman a careful hug. Then she helped her back into the truck, and picked up a shovel.

"Who the hell…decided…that six feet…was a good depth?" Danny panted. She, Kathleen-Rose, and her uncle had already taken brief breaks, and finally he wove his way over to another gravestone and sat down, leaning against it. "Sorry, there," he said, patting the marble. "No disrespect meant."

Vanessa knew she was going to have horrible blisters on her hands later. If they made it that long, she thought, glancing toward the cemetery gates again. Aunt Becca and Joyce were keeping an eye on the perimeter. Baptiste's crew wasn't here yet, but they were coming. If this didn't work…

"You and your daughter go get weapons ready, and keep watch," John said. "They've got to be getting close. Vanessa and I'll finish digging."

"Sounds good," Danny said, giving him a thumbs-up from where he was still leaning against the headstone. "I'll get right to that soon as I can feel my feet again."

"C'mon, dad," Kathleen-Rose said, huffing out a laugh as she took hold of his hands. "Up."

"You see this?" Danny asked. "No respect for her elders."

"They gotta earn it first," Kathleen-Rose teased, and her father grinned at her before digging through the duffel bags, getting everything they had left set out and ready to use.

Then Aunt Becca shouted something. The truck started up right next to them, and Danny and Kathleen-Rose jumped. "What the—" he started, and then Jeanne-Marie drove toward the front of the cemetery, running over several possums that had beaten the main pack here. She hit all but one (and knocked over three tombstones). Joyce hit the straggler with her shovel, and Jeanne-Marie drove back to them, a grim look on her face.

"Hate disturbing graves," she whispered, looking from where she'd knocked into the headstones to where John and Vanessa were over their heads in her mother's grave. "However accidental, or necessary."

"I'm sure whatever spirits or saints or Gods are out there, they'll understand, ma'am," Danny said reassuringly. "Need me to get anything out of the truck for you?"

"My jars, please."

"We hit it!" Vanessa exclaimed, as her exhausted arms finally pushed the shovel into something other than dirt.

"Good. I need the…the box she's holding. But I shouldn't touch it, not until I'm sure the magic's broken. Baptiste cast a powerful spell; if I handle whatever he cursed before it's dealt with, it might never leave."

Feeling sick at that thought, Vanessa finished digging around her side of the coffin, and then looked to her uncle as he put a hand on the clasp.

"I'll get it," he said. It was a pretty simple casket, Vanessa thought—not one of those ridiculously intricate airtight things that'd probably last until the heat death of the universe. So the body wouldn't be as horrifying as Baptiste's had been, would've had time to decay to a harmless skeleton.

It was still a skeleton she didn't want to see.

Kathleen-Rose helped her up out of the grave, starting to peer down curiously as John wrenched the casket open.

"C'mon," Vanessa said. "Better off not looking. Trust me."

Kathleen-Rose started to protest, but then a warning cry from Joyce had all of them grabbing up a weapon—or three, in Danny's case—and running toward the front of the cemetery. John set the box down on the ground above and then pulled himself out of the grave. Jeanne-Marie was sitting several feet away, regarding him calmly, a row of jars open at her side. She motioned to the open grass in front of her, and he slowly got to his feet, setting the box down there.

"Open it," she instructed.

John did so, half-expecting some fanged demon to leap out at him. But nothing moved. He didn't see much— a powder of some sort, a coin…a lock of hair?

"Now go on," she said. "You're too nervous around all this; you'll disrupt my intent. Send Vanessa back to me. She'll do."

He picked up a shovel and ran to where his niece was, jabbing her spear at yet another charging possum. "If we get out of this," she said, "we're moving to Hawaii! *They* don't have possums!" She paused. "Right?"

"You're asking the wrong person," he said, pain twisting in his chest as he saw Sophia, crouched by the cemetery gates, eyeing all of them hungrily. "Go on back. Jeanne-Marie needs you."

She nodded, stabbing another approaching possum before she turned and ran. Behind her, she heard the odd noise of one of the potato guns firing, and then Danny's joyous, "That's what I *thought*!"

Skidding to a stop next to Jeanne-Marie, Vanessa crouched down on the opposite side of the open box. It was a weird-looking thing, several items inside, and tiny mirrors glued to the top, bottom, and sides. "What do I do?" she asked.

"Take out each element in turn, and place it on the ground. Goofer dust." When she didn't immediately move, Jeanne-Marie went on. "The yellowish powder."

Vanessa gingerly picked up the satchel of it, eyeing it before she set it on the ground. "Is that a snake skin?"

"Yes, likely from a rattlesnake. And graveyard dirt, I'm sure."

"Sounds friendly," Vanessa whispered.

"The coin. Is it from the year 1926?"

"Yes," Vanessa said, blinking in surprise at it. "How'd you know?"

"The year we were born. Bound him to the magic, and me to the curse. Now, the lock of hair."

"Probably don't want to think too hard about how he got this."

"No, I don't. The candle."

It was a black candle, with Jeanne-Marie's name carved into it.

"How does—"

She heard a scream—it sounded like Aunt Becca—and started to get to her feet. Jeanne-Marie reached out, quicker than she'd thought she could move, and grab her arm. "You're in this with me now," she said. "We help them by finishing this."

Vanessa bit her lip, but stayed put.

"Break the mirrors," Jeanne-Marie said, and she was more than happy to do that; it meant action, meant doing *something*. She stomped on the box repeatedly, making sure that every one of the mirrors was in tiny shards before she stopped.

Meanwhile, Jeanne-Marie dipped her fingertips into different oils, flicking them over one object and then another as she softly prayed. Once each one was saturated, she looked up at Vanessa. "Still have that lighter?"

"Yes."

"Good. Light the black candle, and burn each of those things."

Vanessa dug the lighter out of her pocket and flicked it on, missing the candle wick on her first three tries because her hands were shaking so badly. Finally, she got it lit, and touched the flame to the satchel of goofer dust.

It burst into flame—which she'd expected, fire touching flammable oil—but the color of the flame was wrong, a deep midnight blue.

She started to say something, but Jeanne-Marie had gone back to her prayers, and it was probably best not to interrupt. She moved on to the coin and the hair—the former of which shouldn't have burned at all, save for maybe the oil coating it. But when the small fire died out, the coin was nowhere to be seen. The hair and the satchel were gone too, not even leaving singe marks on the patch of grass.

"Now what?" she whispered.

"Now we find out if this meant anything," Jeanne-Marie said. She touched her fingertip to some of the dirt they'd tossed out of her mother's grave, and gingerly reached out and rubbed it over where her name was scratched into the candle.

The words disappeared.

"Good. Now, I can hold it," she said, and Vanessa carefully passed it to her. Wrapping both hands around the tapered candle, Jeanne-Marie lowered her mouth closer to it, and blew it out.

Across the cemetery, Vanessa heard shrieks and shouts of alarm.

"Are they all right?" she asked, and this time nothing could've kept her from springing to her feet. "Jeanne-Marie!"

"It's gone," she said dazedly. "It's broken. There's

no more magic here."

Which wasn't exactly an answer, Vanessa thought, and though at any other time she would've helped the older woman to her feet and asked how she was feeling, now she raced past her to where she'd left her family.

Mindless of her hurt arm, Aunt Becca was cradling Sophia on her lap, her uncle crouching next to them both. Sophia no longer bore the fur and teeth, but she wasn't moving.   Vanessa knelt down in front of her, carefully wiping the blood away from her nose. Looked like Kathleen-Rose might've broken it with that kick.

She was breathing. That was something, anyway.

"Hey, Soph," she said. "Come on. Wake up."

"Vanessa?"

She turned, rising to her feet when she saw Tiffany stumbling toward her, looking like she'd just gotten done with a three-day bender.

"Tiffany!" she cried, and threw her arms around her so fiercely that she almost knocked her backward.

"What happened?" Tiffany asked. "What are we doing at the cemetery, why are there dead possums everywhere, and…and who the hell gave the Stewarts potato guns?"

"Built them ourselves, thank you," Danny said proudly.

"You don't remember?" Vanessa asked, pulling back to search her face.

"I remember feeling sick," Tiffany murmured. "I

called in to work. I think I piled every blanket I've ever owned on top of me and then… Ness, what *is* all this?"

"I don't even know how to start explaining," she confessed, and then turned at the sound of Sophia's voice.

"Mom? Dad?"

Both of them pressed closer to hug her, and Vanessa laughed and dropped to her knees, hugging them each in turn.

"This is the weirdest fucking day," Tiffany muttered, sitting down next to them. She glanced around at the rest of the crowd, and then frowned as she saw a figure approaching.

"Is that Kendra's great-grandma?"

"Yeah," Vanessa said, brushing her hand through Sophia's tangled brown curls. "You ever met her?"

"No. Kendra talks about her sometimes."

Vanessa smiled. Jeanne-Marie was walking forward confidently, her cane left behind, no sign of the limp her brother's curse had given her. "She's pretty amazing."

CHAPTER TWELVE

Jeanne-Marie parked her truck in front of her house, smiling as she opened the door. It was an odd emotion, considering everything she'd gone through today—but she felt at peace.

At least until she saw the open chicken coop, looked up, and saw all of her chickens sitting in nearby trees.

She sighed. "Of course."

~~*

"Hi, sweeties!" Sophia said, opening the aquarium without hesitation. "Do you need more food? Yes you do!"

She let them climb up into her hands, while her cousin gaped at her. "How do you do that? I don't ever want to see another possum again and I didn't actually turn into one."

"Not their fault," Sophia said. "Besides, they're all better now. Aren't you, cuties? Yes you are!" The possums who'd still been alive at the cemetery when the spell had been broken had just waddled off, confused. A few of them had played dead when people got too close. There hadn't been a hiss or a growl among them.

Then Vanessa frowned, looking past her. "What happened to your door?"

"Long story," Sophia said. "Can you get the

calcium powder out from under my bed?"

"Yeah," Vanessa said. She did so, and Sophia mixed up a new batch of formula for the babies. Despite their ordeal, they all seemed to be healthy. Good.

In the other room, she could hear her mom and dad talking. They'd decided on a story about straight line winds to explain the phone lines being down and people getting killed.

Her hands trembled a little as she filled the bowl. She didn't know if she was responsible for any of those deaths or not. Vanessa had reassured her, as had her father, telling her that when they'd seen her, it had just been leading the pack around, not hurting anyone herself.

But what would she have done to Kathleen-Rose, if her family hadn't pulled her into the truck?

At first, she hadn't been able to remember a single thing, but as time went on little flashes came and went in her mind. One of those flashes was her grabbing her Kathleen-Rose's ankle, trying her hardest to pull her into the fray. She wondered if Tiffany was getting little flashes, too.

If one of those flashes might show something they couldn't live with.

"Soph?" her mom asked. "You okay?"

"Yeah, yeah," Sophia said, putting the lid back on the aquarium. "I've gotta go to the Stewart's; I'll be right back."

"I'll walk you there."

Sophia started to roll her eyes, to protest that it was just a couple of blocks away, but then she saw the look on her mom's face.

Yeah, she probably wouldn't be going anywhere alone for the next year. Maybe two.

So she said, "Okay!" instead, and walked with her mom. Neither of them said much. She knew that her mom had to have questions—she'd started to ask some at the cemetery, but when she hadn't been able to answer she'd stopped. No point asking yet.

There had been a voice in her head. She hadn't been able to get an image of a face, of an actual physical presence…but when Vanessa had told mom that they'd found Baptiste Broussard dead, she'd burst into tears.

The force of it had shocked even her; she'd cried hysterically for at least ten minutes, unable to stop no matter how much she ordered herself to calm down.

None of her family had seemed surprised, they'd just hugged her and reassured her, and as much as she loved them for that she'd also hated them for a minute or two, wanted to scream at them that she didn't deserve any of that reassurance; even if she hadn't hurt people herself she'd helped animals track them down and do it for her.

In the (very few) werewolf movies she'd been allowed to see, the werewolf always came back to themselves at the urging of someone who loved them. They were strong enough, held on to enough of themselves, to break the spell.

Why hadn't she been able to do that?

Still lost in thought, she walked up to the Stewart's door and knocked, shifting her weight from foot to foot.

Their dad opened the door, and smiled down at her. Well, that was better than the reaction she'd half-expected. "Hi," she said. "Can I talk to Kathleen-Rose?"

"Sure," he said. "C'mon in." He glanced to the sidewalk, where her mom was waiting. "You want to come in, too?" he asked.

"No, that's okay."

He nodded and shut the door behind him, showing her to Kathleen-Rose's room.

She knocked, and the older girl opened the door, looking down at her in surprise. "Hi."

"Hi," she said, trying to remember everything she'd thought about saying to her. "I, um…"

"How's your nose?"

Sophia blinked, startled. She raised her hand to her nose, touched it gingerly. "It's okay. Mom said it didn't quite get broken, but I'm probably gonna have a black eye."

"Sorry about that," Kathleen-Rose said, smiling bashfully.

"What are you apologizing for?" Sophia asked, all of her planned words vanishing in a wave of indignation. "I would've killed you! Or at the very least turned you into a…a were-possum!"

Kathleen-Rose giggled, and Sophia deflated,

realizing how absolutely ridiculous that sounded. Accurate, but ridiculous. "What I mean is, I'm sorry, too."

"It's okay," Kathleen-Rose said. "No harm done."

She hoped so, Sophia thought, as she made her goodbyes and their dad walked her back to the door. She really hoped so. "How's Tim?" she asked, stepping onto the porch. "Dad told me he'd been at the clinic."

"Doing better," he said. "And I'd say I bet he'll think twice before taking another dare, but he won't."

She grinned. "Probably not."

"And hey, Kathleen-Rose is right. Wasn't you. You wouldn't hurt a fly, kid, much less a person."

"Thanks, Mr. Stewart."

~~*

Vanessa stared at her phone, at the number she had up on the screen.

All she had to do was press 'call'.

They'd been so close once, she thought. Now she was getting the shakes just at the idea of hearing his voice again.

Enough, she thought, and tapped the screen before the butterflies in her stomach could turn into bats. Look at what you just went through. You can handle a phone call.

Besides, it had been far too long. There were some things she had to know. Had to be things he wanted to know, too. She'd been so conflicted all these years about contacting him again; what if, all this time, he'd felt the same way? God knew he was impulsive—had quit two jobs during her childhood because of employee mistreatment, once of him and once of a friend of his. He'd told her, when she'd fretted about how they'd buy groceries (and toys. She had, after all, been about ten) he'd hugged her close and told her that they would make it through, that sometimes he acted without thinking and he was sorry those consequences had affected her, too.

What if throwing her out had been the same thing? Her grandma and grandpa were very traditionally Catholic; he went to Mass once or twice a year and joked about being a lapsed Catholic, but what if finding out about her that way had just startled him, thrown him back to some of the stricter elements of his childhood? And then she'd been gone before he could calm down and explain?

She had looked toward Baptiste's house, her eyes drawn irrevocably to that hanging body. She'd seen Jeanne-Marie reach out, tenderly rest her hand on her brother's body despite all that he'd done to her.

If she could forgive every malicious thing he'd done, surely she could reconcile with her father.

Then his voice came through, and she closed her eyes so tightly it hurt.

"Hello?"

"It's me," she managed.

"I know," he said. "Caller ID."

So he still had her number. That meant something,

right? "I just…I guess I just wanted to say hi."

"What for?"

Vanessa sat down on her bed, unsure her knees were willing to support her weight right now. It wasn't the "I'm so glad you called; so happy to hear from you; I'm sorry" that her inner teenager had been not-so-secretly hoping for.

But she'd called him out of the blue, she told herself. A little surprise, a little defensiveness, was to be expected. For all he knew, she'd called him up to scream at him. "Wanted to talk to you again," she said. "It's been a while."

He didn't answer. Her mind racing through too many questions and emotions at once, she lighted on one that she'd been curious about ever since her uncle had come back to the convenience store with her things. "What did Uncle John say?" she asked. "When he came to your house that night?"

Again, there was no answer, and she moved the phone away from her face for a second to make sure he hadn't hung up.

Then, finally, "Does it matter?" he asked, his voice hoarse. From grief or irritation? Time was, she would've known the answer to that right away.

"If that's it," he continued. "Good talking to you."

"I'm getting married!" she exclaimed, before he honestly could close the connection. This was it. "Her name's Tiffany. She's really wonderful." Her throat closed around the words 'I think you'd like her' because, though she wanted to say it, wanted to give him the full benefit of the doubt, a part of her knew. Had known since the moment she'd fled to that convenience store in tears.

"Well," he said, and though she'd braced herself for it, she still winced at the sneer in his voice. "Good for you."

Vanessa thought about what Sophia would say— "Want to come to the wedding? We're going to play pin the tail on the homophobe!" and what Tiffany would say— a beautifully concise "Fuck you". Which would, honestly, be what her aunt would say, too.

Then she thought of what her uncle would say, what even needed to be said anymore, and she just moved the phone away from her ear and pressed 'end'.

Feeling dazed, and still a little weak-kneed, she left her room. The smell of something cooking led her to the kitchen, where Uncle John was making up some grilled cheese sandwiches. She smiled, remembering all the times he'd lightly complained that he had two dozen cookbooks in the house, but all they seemed to want was 'glorified snack food'.

Never stopped him from making it whenever they'd asked.

"Hey," he said, brow furrowing when he took in her expression. "You okay?"

"I called him."

He didn't look confused, not for an instant, and she wondered how long he'd known that this day was coming.

He took the sandwiches out of the pan and turned off the burner, then went to the small kitchen table and patted the seat across from him. "So I'll repeat," he said. "You okay?"

"I think so?" she said. "I guess…I guess I was just expecting something different. He sounded like me calling him was a hassle. I thought, after all this time, maybe…"

"I'm sorry, kiddo."

"Where's Aunt Becca and Sophia?"

"She wanted to go talk to Kathleen-Rose." He was silent for a moment, and then he went on, his voice low and hesitant. "You've asked, before, what we said to each other that night. I never answered—no, more than that, I brushed you off—and maybe I shouldn't have. But you were having nightmares all the time, and your grades… I guess I thought if I pretended that it didn't matter anymore, you'd stop focusing on it, too."

And on some days, Vanessa thought, that had worked. But other days, it just felt like an infection was spreading, that she couldn't find a way to lance it and let the poison out.

"When I got to his house," he said, after she didn't protest, didn't tell him she'd changed her mind, "he was packing your things. Some were…were already out at the curb. I asked him, what the fuck do you think you're doing?"

If Vanessa hadn't been sitting down, she might've toppled right over. She'd never, in her life, heard him swear. Not even when he was playing video games with

Sophia, something that tested even Aunt Becca's legendary non-temper.

Seemingly unaware that she was gaping, he went on, his words as toneless and rushed as a sixth-grader forced to read in front of the class. "He said that you were moving out. That he was disowning you. I told him you were coming to stay with us. He said that was our choice, but that as long as we were…were 'harboring' you, he wouldn't come visit."

"Did you tell him that wouldn't be much loss?" Vanessa asked, trying for a smile.

"No, but I should have. Too mad to think straight, I guess," he said. "I just told him to shut up and help me get your things to the car, if he was so sure this was what he wanted. I thought that carrying out your graduation cap, pictures of the two of you together, your favorite stuffed animal when you were a kid…I thought it'd make him stop. Make him *think*. But he just helped ferry everything out. Without another word."

"Those checks," she finally said. "The ones you told me he sent every month to help take care of me. They didn't exist, did they?"

He shook his head. "Becca and I thought it might be easier if there was something to help ease the transition, rather than saying…"

"…that he was just that much of a dick?"

That startled a laugh out of him. "Language," he said fondly.

She smiled and then barreled ahead, unwilling to put this off and risk losing her courage. "I told you Tiffany and I are getting married next Friday." 'Screw the rings', Tiffany had told her. "We'll buy those later. I want to be able to call you my wife *now*.' "And I, um…I know that it's kindof an outdated tradition, and it's not something I ever really pictured doing, but…"

Get it out, Vanessa thought, as he raised an eyebrow at her.

"Anyway, I…I'd really like it if you would walk me down the aisle. Dad."

He just stared at her, and for a few seconds she was afraid she'd somehow messed something up. She was too keyed-up and emotional to think straight and she'd accidentally said something wrong, she'd—

Then he got to his feet, hauling her up and into his arms, hugging her so tightly that her feet actually left the ground and she was pretty sure her ribcage creaked.

"Hey now," she laughed, hugging him back. "Watch it. No cracked ribs at my wedding."

EPILOGUE

Trevor flipped back and forth between Netflix and Hulu and Amazon, groaning when he couldn't seem to find anything he wanted to watch.

He had one hell of an excuse for lounging around for a while—infection had set in to some of the bites on his right leg, and it had gotten so bad so quickly that they'd had no choice but to amputate.

Now he was back home, but there was nobody to come home to. The Chief of Police had stopped by a few times, checking in; so had Miss Broussard.

He'd been glad when she left. She gave him the creeps. Sounded like if she'd just swallowed her pride and reconciled with her brother, none of this would've happened at all.

They hadn't found Sam's body yet. But it was now considered gospel truth that she'd been one of the first victims.

Which boiled down to the same problem Miss Broussard had, he thought. If Sam had just gotten over it—it was a *word*, for God's sake. Not the nicest one, sure, but she hadn't needed to storm off.

He just hoped Alexis didn't try to visit again. She'd come to see him as he was getting into the ambulance that'd take him to Parsons, the town with the nearest good-sized hospital.

"I'm sorry," she'd said. "About running."

He'd almost snapped at her, almost yelled, told her that it didn't matter whether she was sorry or not, she'd left all of them to die.

Not that she would've been able to do anything against the horde that had flooded into that trailer, he reminded himself. But still.

"Don't worry about it," he'd said instead. "What's done is done."

She hadn't looked reassured, but he couldn't bring himself to care. She'd hopped out a window and taken off for greener pastures, and now everyone else was dead. Including Alexis's boyfriend.

Jesus, he thought, Caleb would've done anything for her. And she hadn't even had the decency to at least *try* to help him?

No, he definitely didn't want her to come back.

A scraping noise from the front room had him turning his head. His neighbor, Paula, had volunteered to come by twice a day and feed his cat until he got better with moving around on his own. She also brought him food sometimes, which was nice.

But she wasn't scheduled to come by for another hour.

"Hello?" he called, grabbing his crutches and gingerly getting to his feet.

Foot.

"Goddammit," he muttered. "Hello?"

A familiar figure moved into the doorway—the blonde hair was caked with leaves and mud; normally-pristine clothes were torn and filthy, but it was still unmistakably *her*. "Sam," he breathed. "Oh, babe, I'm so glad to see you. We all thought you were dead!"

Then she came closer, further into the light from the open curtains, and his face drained of color.

She was torn open, bites and claw marks all over her, some of them scabbed up and some still oozing blood. Parts of her skull were visible. A flap of skin dangled from her jaw, and he found himself irrationally focused on that for a few precious seconds until he heard claws scrabbling across the floor and looked down.

She'd brought friends.

Trevor glanced toward the back door, a reflex more than an honest hope. He knew he'd never make it in time.

Sam moved closer, smiling—she couldn't help but smile, not really, most of her lips were gone—and he tried to retreat and just ended up falling right back into his chair as she advanced on him.

"Well, fuck."

~~*

"…is that what I think it is?"

Danny grinned at her. "I believe the line is, 'Is that a potato gun in your pocket, or are you just happy to see me?'"

Vanessa laughed. "I suppose I should just be glad you didn't bring the flamethrowers. But still—to a wedding?"

"Better to have it and not need it—"

"—than need it and not have it, I know." Smiling ruefully, Vanessa gave him a hug.

"Careful, now, don't smush your corsage," he said, and then looked to the buffet set up at the right side of the room. "Don't suppose John made some of those brown butter cookies?"

"He did. And we've got a box for you in the car," Vanessa whispered.

"You're all saints."

Vanessa laughed, and then her eyes widened as she saw Timmy, who was currently trying to hop from the back of one pew to the next, cheerfully making bets with his older siblings as to how far he could get.

"If that boy doesn't end today by getting dental work…" Danny muttered. "Tim! Get on down from there!"

As he went to his son, Vanessa walked over to Tiffany. Her new wife smiled, the sheer joy in the expression bringing tears to her eyes.

"Hey now, none of that," Tiffany said, pulling her close for a kiss. "You know how many times I had to redo this mascara to make it look nice? Can't ruin it now."

They looked to Jeanne-Marie then, who was talking very animatedly to Leanne Perkins, the owner of the town funeral home.

"What do you mean it wasn't working?"

"I told you, Miss Broussard, it was out of my control. I just—"

"And I told you what to—" she began, pausing when Vanessa and Tiffany closed the distance between them.

"What's going on?" Tiffany asked.

"This idiot didn't cremate him!"

"As I was explaining to Miss Broussard," Leanne said, her voice and expression gone cold, "I did everything I could to cater to her wishes. But my cremator stopped working. I have someone coming to repair it next week. Her poor brother's body was already in…less than ideal condition, so I made a judgment call."

"You made a call that's going to end with me shutting you down, that's what you did!"

"Please lower your voice," Leanne said. "This is a day of joy and community togetherness, not—"

"I'm all right with her making a scene if that's what she thinks is necessary," Tiffany said, looking to Vanessa and getting a nod of confirmation.

"Can't he be exhumed after your cremator's fixed?" Vanessa asked.

"If it's really that important to her, then yes," Leanne sniffed. "Though if she'd bothered to come to her brother's burial service, she'd already know about—"

"Please leave," Tiffany said. They hadn't bothered with invitations—after everything that had happened, they'd just passed the word along that the wedding would be held in the town's largest church, with a community potluck afterward as a reception. Most everyone in town was in attendance and, until now, that had been fine.

"Well," Leanne said. "I…I'm taking my scalloped potatoes back."

"Feel free," Tiffany said.

Leanne marched over to the buffet table and picked up her dish, then stalked out of the church.

"Everything okay?" Aunt Becca asked, coming over to them with John and Sophia at her side.

"Yeah," Vanessa said. "Leanne was just being a jerk. Is it legal to bury someone when their next of kin wants them cremated, or vice versa?"

Her aunt frowned. "You know, I'm not sure, not when it comes to those kinds of laws. I can look into it, though. Miss Jeanne-Marie, are you wanting to—"

Then she flinched, her good hand reaching for a gun that she wasn't wearing today when Leanne screamed outside.

"Wait here," she told the others, dodging the crowd to head for the front door. Before she could get there, it was flung open.

Sam stood there, a young raccoon perched on her shoulder and at least a dozen others behind her. Their muzzles were red with blood.

"Dad…" Sophia said, as she caught sight of a raccoon's face peering in one of the windows. As she watched, it raised one of its eerily human-like hands and scratched its fingernails down the glass.

"Kids!" Melanie Stewart shouted, as her husband and eldest son reached under their seats and pulled out potato guns. "You know what to do!"

"Sophia," John said. "Hide behind the podium." Then he grabbed a large wooden crucifix from where it stood on a display table near the front of the church, giving the startled minister an apologetic smile before running to his wife's side.

"C'mere," Tiffany said, grabbing Vanessa's hand and leading her to the centerpiece of the buffet, their wedding cake. She grabbed the sharp knife that was lying beside it.

"Don't have time for a pretty toast," she said, as Sam let out an animalistic shriek and the raccoons charged. Their townsfolk kicked them away or hit them with the Bibles that had been nestled behind each pew, as the Stewarts let loose with their potato guns. Tiffany cut a tiny piece of cake, broke it in half, and held one piece out for Vanessa to eat, popping the other into her own mouth.

Vanessa smiled at her, then grabbed a large serving fork from one of the casseroles. "Cemetery?" she called to Jeanne-Marie. The older woman nodded.

"Hey, Ness!" Danny shouted, as he took out a raccoon with a well-aimed vegetable missile. "You want to tease me about our potato guns now?"

"Never again," Vanessa called, grabbing one of the

tall candle stands and swinging at a raccoon that was charging at her feet. "Come with us to the cemetery?"

Danny groaned. "We got to dig up somebody else?"

"Afraid so!"

"Suppose I can ride along," he said, discarding the potato gun in favor of yanking one of the tapestries off the wall and flinging it over three raccoons, confusing them long enough for John to hit them repeatedly with the cross. "After all, hate for you two to get those pretty dresses dirty!"

Vanessa let out a panicky laugh, and Tiffany skewered a raccoon that had leaped onto the buffet table and then wrapped an arm around her shoulders. "If our wedding is this weird," she said, "I can't wait for the honeymoon."

ABOUT THE AUTHOR

Stephanie is a queer, glitter-obsessed, sleep-deprived mother of two with about five hundred projects. Some are actually completed, and available now!

Pale Moon: Elspeth Jansen's life turns upside-down when she rescues a wounded puppy, only to find out that the puppy is actually a young werewolf. A queer, polyam romance/found family novel.

Short Story Collections (all proceeds go to RAICES):
Last Petal on the Rose and Other Stories
Desert Journey and An Uncommon Road
Angels with Clipped Wings and Other Stories

Keep up to date at stephanierabig.weebly.com, or say hello on Twitter @stephrabig!

TRIGGER WARNINGS

- violence against animals
- emotionally abusive parent